THE CARDINAL'S SONG

BOOK THREE OF ALVIN'S JOURNEY
J.E. McCARTHY

West Front Media, LLC

The Cardinal

by T.M. Moore

    The cardinal perched a moment in his day
and flashed his bright red overcoat my way.
Against the backdrop of the shadows and the leaves
and needles, dark green in this stand of woods,
he flamed out momentarily
as he flitted back and forth in front of me.
Then he was gone.
I only glimpsed him,
just like many other glory tokens
thrust before me day by day,
reminders of an omnipresent,
always-working love that never fails.
That love can bring delight
when ordinary things that catch my sight,
and show themselves in heightened ways
lead me to wonder, joy, and grateful praise.

One

T he New Year's Day feast was magnificent. It was a boiled dinner with a massive ham. Catherine and Mary had made minced meat pies from venison, and something called a *tourtiere* pie that the French Canadians ate. It was Mary's sixteenth birthday complete with a carrot cake and whipped cream. Alvin loved that cake because of the spices. It reminded him of home. By the end of the meal, he stretched out by the fire and closed his eyes. His mind had drifted into a dream when he felt Arthur poke him in the ribs.

"Will you take a drink?" asked Arthur.

Alvin opened his eyes wide. "I'll take some tea or coffee."

Arthur laughed. "Good God man. When I was your age, I'd drink for three days and three nights and not miss a minute of work."

"What did you do for work?"

"I delivered coal. Of course, I didn't always get the right house being in a state of drink, but I was there on time." Arthur laughed and slapped his knee.

Alvin grinned. "Well, my cow is probably full to bursting and she needs me to get down there soon."

"Well, when you come back, bring me some butter. I like yours better than ours. Or just send some back with Mary."

"I will." Alvin started to rise from his chair.

Arthur looked around and raised a hand to stop him. He leaned forward and whispered. "Is she bothering you? Being down there so much?"

Alvin sat back down and shook his head. "No. I enjoy the company and honestly, she knows more about farming than I do."

"Here's the thing. Her mother thinks it's not good for her. She has the impression that Mary is in love with you. It's always Alvin this and Alvin that. Whenever Catherine mentions a woman for you, Mary gets cross and explains the woman's faults, like she's jealous."

Alvin shrugged and scratched his chin, but didn't speak.

"I don't notice these things, but women do." Arthur sat back in his chair. "I guess what I'm trying to say is that young girls are impressionable. Hell, young boys too for that matter. Kevin and Daniel are worse than her sometimes. I just don't want to see her heart get broken."

Alvin felt a gnawing in his gut. He would never want to break her heart, he loved her. As much as he had loved Edna. "I understand. I treasure her above all things."

Arthur smiled and gave one great nod. "Excellent. You're good lad."

Alvin felt a sense of guilt wash over him. Arthur was his friend and had treated him like a son. Better actually, he never called Alvin by girl's names or made japes at his expense. Now Alvin had taken his daughter's virginity and far more than that. It didn't feel like lust or youthful passion to him. It felt like it was meant to be. There were times when he held her that he literally could not get close enough to her. He wanted to feel every inch of her pressing against him. It made him feel calm. It made him feel loved.

January brought cold and snow. Lots of snow. Alvin kept the animals in the barn and his routine was now centered around feeding and watering. He rose in the dark and milked, then came back around at sunset to do it again. He missed sitting on the porch to read and the house felt massive and empty. He had confined his living to a couple of rooms downstairs to save on firewood and really didn't have a use for the rest of it yet.

He spent his days between milking with moving snow, but it seemed as soon as he would have the dooryard cleared, they would have another storm or the cold winds whipping around Howell hill would drift new snow onto his driveway and he'd have to start the process all over again.

The kitchen was his favorite room, and the stove gave off enough heat to keep it warm. When he was done his chores, he liked to sit in an old rocking chair and read while he drank tea or coffee. Alvin had picked up the chair and a small side table at an auction and they had become his favorite additions to the house. Throughout the morning, the light was brilliant through the kitchen windows, and he had a perfect view of the lilac tree. Mary had showed him how to make suet with seeds embedded in it and he watched as the birds swooped in and pecked away until they had their fill and swooped off again, only to be replaced by a new bird.

Once when visiting Monroe, he stopped into Smith's Books and Stationary store to buy a pen and paper for letters. Opened on the shelf was a book by John J. Audubon with a beautiful picture of a Red crested bird on a branch and a brown one on the branch below. He picked it up and flipped through the pages. It contained hundreds of pictures of birds and described their habitats. It was called The Birds of America, and he had to have it.

The man who ran the store had been a teacher and half the store was dedicated to books and the other half to stationary. "Do you study ornithology?" asked a large balding man with a broad chest and half rimmed glasses that rested in the middle of his nose.

"I don't. That is to say, I don't study it. But birds fascinate me."

"Then that's the book for you. May I?" He took the book from Alvin and opened to the title page and pointed to a signature. "This book was signed by Audubon himself. It's not an original. This is a reprint from 1850. The man died a year or so later."

Alvin looked at the book binding. The leather was cracking, and the page edges seemed water stained. "How much?"

Smith smiled. "A dollar. I couldn't let it go for less than that."

Alvin thought for a moment and smiled back. "I'll take it." He hadn't planned on buying a book and a dollar was a fair sum of money to him, but something about the book spoke to him."

"Excellent. Come over here." Smith walked behind the counter and started to write a receipt. "What's your name son?"

"Alvin McGinn. You?"

"I'm Gordon Smith. Some people call me Gordie and a few call me professor, although I never taught at a university. But most people around here never went to school past the age of fourteen, so I guess I'm a professor to them."

Alvin paid him and hurried back to the farm as quickly as he could to start reading the book right away.

Now as he read other books and smoked his pipe, he watched the lilac tree and the suet cake dangling to see what species came to visit. At first, he has thought about writing the date of each sighting in the book itself but decided that was too much risk of getting ink on the pages, so he kept a list on paper. The winter brought a nearly continuous flow of birds and in one morning he once saw ten different bird species.

He sat watching a Bluejay and its mate pecking at the suet from each side of the cake and it seemed to swing back and forth like some game. It swung to the male and it took a few pecks and then to the female for her turn. He watched them eat their fill and disappear in a blue flash. His eyes were drawn past the tree, and he saw Mary hurrying up the driveway with a basket. Her face was covered with a scarf and only her eyes were really visible.

Alvin stood and met her at the door. When he opened it, a biting cold wind slapped him in the face and the moment she was in, he slammed the door shut.

Mary unwrapped her head and her cheeks and nose were bright red in spite of the scarf. "It's so cold!" She pulled her mittens from her hands and held them a few inches off from the kitchen stove. "I could lay on this right now. I'm frozen to my bones."

Alvin stepped behind her and wrapped his arms around hers. "I'll warm you up," He whispered and held her tighter, and she laid her head back to press her cheek to his.

They stood like that for a minute, and he released her. "What's in the basket?"

"Ham and minced meat pie. Mam said to eat it before it goes bad. Daddy wants me to bring back butter too."

Alvin stood beside her and warmed his hands as well. "He mentioned that to me. Along with some other things."

"He did?" she asked.

"It appears that your mother thinks you're in love with me, and he doesn't want to see you get your heart broken." Alvin looked at Mary to judge her reaction.

She shrugged. "Don't break my heart then."

Alvin laughed. "I hope you know; I'd never do anything to cause you pain."

Mary sighed. "I do and she is right. I do love you...how do you say I love you in Irish?"

Alvin scratched his head. "The words aren't the same. We don't say it like that, we say *A chuisle mo chroi*"

"What does that mean?"

Alvin took her hand and placed it on his chest. "O pulse of my heart...It means you make my heart, beat."

Two

Alvin was told that the end of January and the first weeks of February were the coldest in Maine. He found it difficult to tell the difference. From New Years Day through January, the temperature never rose above freezing. Even the days with cloudless skies brought bitter winds down from the North. The farm was situated on the south side of Howell Hill, which Arthur said helped cut down on the wind, but Alvin listened to it howl night after night like some hungry wolf looking for a way in and the coldest part of his day was always the trips to and from the barn to tend the animals.

He still worked the ponies three or four days a week to keep them fit, but the workdays were kept short in the woods from the lack of sun in the afternoons. He liked working in the cedar swamp in the winter because the ground was frozen and made twitching wood much faster than the rest of the year. He was cutting fence posts for his own property to give the animals more room to roam and he was considering a beef critter this year and wanted to be able to keep it away from Bessy, which was the name he had given his cow. There might be a time when he wanted her to mate, but he had more food than he had ever known in his life and the thought of milking two cows twice a day was more than he wanted to contemplate.

Alvin lifted a long cedar tree onto his saw rack and began cutting posts with his bow saw. He had learned early on that if he could cut with both hands, he didn't tire as easily, so each cut was made with the opposite hand from the first one. In the beginning, the left-hand cuts were slow and sloppy, but as time went on, he felt like he was as close to ambidextrous as he would ever be.

Despite the cold, the work and his layers of clothing kept him warm. The trick was not to stop for too long. Once the sweat cooled, that's when the chill crept in. He sawed post after post and laid them neatly on a pile. His work was disrupted by the hoofbeats of a horse coming from Monroe. It was a single rider, and he waved to Alvin.

Alvin squinted across the brilliant snow and the glare from the sun made it hard to see, but it looked like Parker Moreland. He laid down his saw and made his way to the yard.

Parker wore a coat of heavy fur and a fur hat to match. The black fur seemed to shine like cut coal in the winter sun. Parker rode into the yard and dismounted. "Where can I tie him up?" he asked.

Alvin pointed to a split-rail fence that had once been part of the pasture. Parker tied the big Morgan and pulled a package from the saddlebag. "My father asked me to bring this to you." And handed him a parcel wrapped in paper and tied with a string.

Alvin felt the weight in his hands. "What is it?"

Parker shrugged. "Haggis, I think. They were making some this morning."

"Haggis? Been a fair bit since I've had any of that," said Alvin.

"I'm not fond of it myself. But my grandmother was from the Highlands, so they ate it pretty regular growing up. The Scotts don't waste anything you know."

Alvin nodded. "That's a sound practice. If you had to tend the damned thing, you might as well get all you can out of it. Thank him for me, or better yet, if you have a minute, I'll write him a note. Would you be caring for some tea or coffee?"

Parker stood for a long moment just looking around the farm. His bright blue eyes somehow seemed to have lost their luster. Alvin knew that look all too well.

"I'll take some coffee, or something stronger if you have it."

Alvin motioned to the house. "Come on in. I always have something stronger, if you can stomach the poteen. It's like drinking turpentine, but it gets the job done."

"Maybe just coffee then."

They went inside and the heat felt like a welcomed relief. Alvin threw some wood into the kitchen stove and opened the dampers. Within minutes, the crackles of the fire could be heard while Alvin prepared the coffeepot. "Biscuits?"

Parker shook his head. "No, I had lunch already. Thank you, though."

Parker looked at the ashtray and pipe on the table, then pulled a metal box from his pocket and lit a cigarette. "And thank you for not asking me how I am doing."

Alvin understood immediately. That question had set his teeth on edge for the months following the loss of Edna and Nora. Alvin opened his cupboard and reached into the back. He pulled a bottle and inspected the contents. "I have a little Canadian Whiskey here. Will that serve?"

Parker exhaled and nodded. "Perfectly."

Alvin placed two glasses on the table and poured them each a drink. He held his glass up to Parker, "Slainte," and took a sip.

Parker took a drink of his whiskey and placed the glass on the table. "What's that mean?"

"Health."

Parker chuckled quietly to himself and shook his head. "Health, I have. I wife I don't."

"It's a hard place to be."

"I think my father sent me here with that Haggis, so I'd talk with you. He's growing tired of me snapping at everyone and walking around with a scowl on my face."

"How long have he and your mother been married?"

"Nearly thirty years now. He was almost forty when they met. Why do you ask?"

"Well, I'd never wish it on anyone, but if he lost her, he'd understand the scowling."

11

Parker laughed a little at that and took another sip of the whiskey. "I don't know where to go from here. We have a maid to care for the boy and my younger sister dotes on him. But I don't know anything about raising a child."

Alvin took another drink and thought on that for a moment. "I suspect it's something you just learn along the way. I'm sure I don't know a thing about it either except you feed em and change their nappy when it's soiled and eventually, they walk and talk and then you can work with them."

"Christ, McGinn. It sounds like you're tending a barn animal. I suspect there's more to it than that."

Alvin stood and removed the coffeepot from the stove and poured two cups. He placed them on the table and poured the rest of his whiskey into his and Parker did the same. "You're probably right."

"How did you handle it? When your wife passed."

Alvin took a deep breath. "Poorly." He sipped his coffee and held the cup in his hands to gain the warmth. "First, I took to drink. Somewhere along the way I realized that I could never drink enough to fill that hole inside me."

Parker snuffed out his cigarette and lit another. "How'd you end up here?"

"My wife father took me aside and set me straight. He told me a story about a friend of his who lost two boys while they were out fishing and told me to turn my mind to something else."

Parker scoffed. "That's easy to say when he's not spending every waking moment is spent longing for what he lost."

"I thought the same thing, too. But the best advice I got was to stop looking back. Focus forward. No amount of wishing will bring them back. It doesn't mean we forget them; we just bring them along in our hearts as we move forward."

Parker thought about that for a moment and nodded. "I don't see a way forward right now."

Alvin lit his pipe and took a long drag then blew the smoke in the air. "What made you happy before she passed, other than being with her, of course."

"Land, I guess. I always feel good when we purchase more land or part of a business. That doesn't last, though. Sometimes it's months between purchases."

Alvin smiled. "I think that's your answer. Turn your mind to your business. I found when I was feeling melancholy, any time I was planning or building something, it brought my mind to the task at hand and not ruminating in the past."

Parker poured some more whiskey into his coffee and took a long drink. He smoothed the hairs of his mustache from hip lips and stared at Alvin. "How old are you?"

"Twenty-five. Why?"

"You have a way of seeming much older. Wiser I guess."

Alvin laughed. "I don't know about all that. I do plenty of foolish things, so I guess the wisdom comes and goes."

Parker drained his coffee and stood. "I have to get back. I appreciate your counsel. You cook that Haggis for about three hours. Don't let it burst, or you'll have a foul stew."

Alvin stood and shook his hand. "Thank you and thank your father. I forgot about the note."

Parker slipped back into his furs and gloves. "I will."

"Come back when it's warmer and we can sit on the porch and talk about land and how you look for it."

"I'll see you in April then," he said with a forced chuckle. He looked like he wanted to say something more, but he just nodded and left.

As he rode out of the yard, he made a motion like he was tipping his hat to someone and turned toward his home. A moment later, Mary walked around the massive snow drift with her hands tucked deep into a deerskin muff and her head wrapped in a thick scarf.

I don't think I'm getting anymore work done today, he thought.

Three

M ary met Alvin in the yard. Her cheeks and nose were red from the battering wind. "Was that Parker Moreland?"

"Yes, his father sent me some Haggis."

Mary scrunched her face and clutched her stomach. "Eww. Just the thought of it is making my stomach revolt."

"It's not that bad. No worse than boiled sheep's head."

Mary grimaced. "Please Alvin. I'm going to puke if you mention another disgusting food."

"What about biscuits?"

"Biscuits are fine. Do you have any?"

Alvin motioned to the house. "Inside."

"Good. I need to warm up."

They stepped into the kitchen and tobacco smoke still hung in the air. Mary hung her coat and sat down, trying not to vomit. "My God, I don't know what's worse the wind or the smoke."

Alvin brought a plate of biscuits and a block of butter to the table. "What's wrong? Are you unwell?"

Mary looked up at him with her brown eyes and sighed. "I've been sick to my stomach lately...In the mornings, mostly."

Alvin sat buttering a biscuit, trying to contemplate a cause when he finally realized what she was saying. "In the morning, you say?"

Mary nodded without smiling. "Yes."

"How long?"

"Since the beginning of February."

Alvin dropped the biscuit and knife and stared at her, trying to gauge her state of mind. "Are you with child?" He couldn't tell if she was going to smile or cry, but he could tell the answer already.

"I am."

Alvin reached over and hugged her. "I'm happy if you are," he whispered.

Mary pushed back from him, and her eyes were filled with tears. "It's *all* I want. You're *all* I want."

Alvin smiled and looked at her watery eyes. "Me too. You're all I want." He kissed her and pulled back again. "I'm yours. Whatever's left of me when your father get's done giving me a hiding."

Mary shook her head and crossed herself. "He's going to be so cross. I'm fearful of what he might do. I thought about telling my mam and having her give him the news."

Alvin shook his head. "That won't do. I'll tell him myself. I did it, so I'll own it."

Mary sat back in her chair and looked at him. "What if he kills you?"

Alvin laughed. "He won't. He might have your brothers do it, but he won't."

"Don't joke about it Alvin. He's like a volcano when he's angry."

Alvin took her hands and kissed her again. "This is a happy day. Not a day for fretting. He'll be angry. But he'll have a grandchild. You were going to marry and have a family someday, so why not with me?"

Mary smiled and wiped her eyes. "Are you honestly happy?"

"I couldn't be happier if I were twins."

It had been two weeks since Mary had given him the news about their coming child, and he agonized over how he would break the news to Arthur. He had thought about waiting until they were both drunk, but he needed his wits about him to handle Arthur's reaction in case he became violent. His salvation came in the form of a letter.

Richard had written to say he'd be in Boston on business in April and would take a train to Monroe to visit. Alvin had corresponded with him a few times over the past year and every return letter came with a promise to visit and now he was actually coming. Arthur had always held a hatred for the English, but

Alvin's stories about Richard had made Artur curious about a man that had done so much for Alvin.

He saddled Buddy and packed a basket with butter and a bottle of Canadian Whiskey he got from the Morelands and rode toward the McCalls. The sun felt good on his face and the snows had receded drastically in the last half of February. He rode along and his ears picked up a loud bird song in the air. He stopped the horse and scanned the tree line searching for its source. His eyes were drawn to a bright red bird with a crest like a Bluejay. Its back face and orange beak stood out in the sunlight. It was a gorgeous cardinal.

He heard a return call and a moment later a tan cardinal landed on a branch not far away. I'll have to add them to my list, he thought. Alvin listened carefully and then tried to mimic the calls by whistling. Both birds sat in silence and the singing stopped. "I must have offended them," he said and started Buddy on his way again. As he passed, he watched them both and admired the simple beauty of them both.

He approached the McCall's farm and met Kevin and Daniel on the road. "Good morning lads. Where are you off to?"

Kevin pulled the wagon to a stop. "On our way to pick up grain and oats."

"What kind of mood is Arthur in today?"

Daniel shrugged. "His usual mood I suppose. He hasn't started drinking yet, so he's his usual irritable self. He'll be happy to see you though. Makes him feel like he's back in Ireland."

"It may be cold here, but he forgets how much it rains there."

Kevin smiled. "Well, have him in a good mood by the time we get back. I don't want to listen to his griping about how long it takes for us to get to Hemming's and back."

Alvin shrugged. "Can't make any promises."

Kevin and Daniel rode on and Alvin made his way to the McCall's.

Buddy walked at his usual plodding pace into the McCall's yard. "It'd be faster to walk on foot as slow as that animal moves." He heard Arthur call form the porch.

Alvin dismounted and tied Buddy to a post. "I think you're right. He's a miserable son of a bitch. But he pulls good in the woods."

"What have you got in your poke?"

Alvin reached into the bag. "Butter... and this." He pulled the whiskey bottle and held it in the air.

"Ah. Water of life. Where'd you get that?"

"Parker Moreland sold me some. He doesn't care for the poteen."

Arthur laughed, "Fancy folks usually don't. Come sit with me."

Alvin climbed the steps to the porch and sat in the chair closest to the stairs. He felt it was fortuitous in case he needed to run get away in a hurry. "I saw the boys, where are Mary and Cat?"

"Up the road to Mrs. Murphys, left me here with barely a morsel to eat. But now that I have your butter at least I can have some bread." Arthur reached into a wooden box and produced two tin cups he used for drinking on the porch.

Alvin poured them each a drink and told him the story of Richard's coming visit. Arthur was in good spirits and didn't even bother to launch into of his rants about his hatred for the English. It made Alvin feel a little guilty for what he was about to do.

"Another drink?" Alvin asked after pouring a little into his cup.

"Of course. I don't drink fine Canadian every day," he said with a smile.

Alvin poured Arthur's drink and corked the bottle.

"Arthur. I have a bit of news you need to hear."

Arthur's affect changed from mirth to concern. "Not bad news from home?"

Alvin shook his head. "No, no. Nothing like that." Alvin paused trying to think of the best way to tell him. He had rehearsed it a thousand times in his head and every scenario ended with Arthur choking him to death. Finally, he took a deep breath and exhaled. "Mary is with child."

"My Mary?" he asked as if there might have been another Mary somewhere he didn't know about.

"Yes."

Arthur sat in silence and Alvin watched as his face flushed with anger as he turned the news in his mind. "How do you know this? Did she tell you?"

"She did. I'm the father," he said and moved slowly to prepare to bolt.

Arthur stared at Alvin in disbelief in a long moment before speaking. "You said you treasure her above all things."

"I do."

Arthur gritted his teeth. "But you defiled her. A child?"

"A young woman, and I want to marry her and have a family with her, you said not to break her heart, and I won't" Alvin replied and felt his muscles tense in a way that he had to fight from running.

"Don't twist my words, you knew what I meant, and it wasn't marriage. There'll be no marriage. Now get off my fucking property. Take the road back to your place. Before I make up my mind to get my shotgun and shoot you dead as good Friday right here in my dooryard."

"Arth..."

Arthur held up a hand and pointed to the road. "Go now. There'll be no marriage."

Alvin wanted to say something else, but Arthur's face was now red with fury, and he started to look as if he was going to rise. Alvin wasn't afraid of taking a beating, but he would never raise a hand to a man that had done so much for him. So, he rose and walked down the porch steps and remounted Buddy. Alvin glanced back, and Arthur was still in his chair just glaring at Alvin. When he caught Alvin's eyes, he scowled and pointed to go. Alvin felt his heart sink. Thay was the look of betrayal. Alvin turned Buddy and quietly clicked his tongue. "Let's go."

Buddy walked out of the yard at so slow of a pace that it served to heighten the guilt and humiliation of having betrayed a friend.

Alvin didn't go home. Instead, he made his way to the Murphy's house to warn Catherine and Mary what they would be coming home to. Alvin and Mary told Catherine the news together. He could see the deep disappointment on her face. She sat in silence for a full minute and Alvin felt his guts going to jelly with anticipation at her response.

Finally, she looked at them both then spoke. "You're not the first two young people to fall into this mess. You won't be the last. You'll need to marry as soon as possible, so Mary won't have a wedding dress with a belly out to here," she said and held a hand from her stomach.

"Arthur says I can't marry her."

"Nonsense. He's just angry. I'll bring him around."

Mary gave a timid smile. "Thank you, Mam."

Catherine frowned. "Don't thank me. I didn't want this for you. You made your bed; now you'll lay in it."

Mary frowned back. "We love each other."

"I'm certain you do. Alvin you're a fine man and Arthur always said he wanted Mary to find a man like you. I just don't think he meant *literally you* and certainly not this way."

Mary dropped her head. "I'm sorry, Mam."

"Me too," added Alvin.

Catherine looked at them and sighed. "It'll be alright. Arthur just needs time."

Four

A few days passed and Alvin had no word from Mary. Whenever the boys passed, they waved but didn't stop. When Arthur passed, he didn't even bother to wave. He just looked forward and drove the horses in anger past the farm.

Every time he saw Arthur drive by, he had contemplated trying to ride to the McCalls and see her but felt it would be more trouble for Mary if he were ever caught.

A week had passed, and Phillip stopped while Alvin was cutting wood. "How goes the battle?" he asked with a grin peeking out from beneath his thick mustache.

"I'm fine. I think Arthur might come down here and murder me in my bed, so I lock up tight at night."

Phillip laughed. "He offered me five dollars to kick the ever-loving shit out of you. But I wouldn't take it."

Alvin smiled and shook his head. "Well, I appreciate that. Five dollars is a reasonable sum. Not easy to turn down."

"I told him the price is ten, but you know how cheap he is."

Both men laughed at that. Then Alvin sighed. "He hasn't let her come down at all."

Phillip put his hand on Alvin's shoulder. "She says she loves you and says you should talk to Arthur anyway. He won't make his grandchild an orphan. She says he barely speaks to her, just glares."

"Thank you, Phil. I appreciate the message."

"You want to say something to her? I'll tell her."

Alvin smiled. "I do. Tell her I love her, and I started working on a crib for the baby. That should make her happy."

Phillip nodded and patted him on the shoulder. "I believe that will. Go see Arthur."

"I will tomorrow. He already passed by here twice today and didn't even look into the yard."

The next morning, Alvin walked to the McCalls with a parcel of butter and some extra eggs. He had far more than he would ever eat.

He climbed the steps to the McCall farm and was about to knock on the door. Arthur met him and stood, blocking his entry.

"What do you want?" he said in a tone like a growl.

"I'd like to see Mary and I have butter and eggs."

Arthur frowned. "We have butter and eggs, feed them to the pigs." He started to shut the door.

"What about Mary?"

Arthur leaned out, looming over Alvin. "I think you've seen enough of her, don't you? I'm sending her to a convent after she has this child. There's one right in Watertown."

Alvin didn't believe that he would actually send her to a convent, but he could see that Arthur was more hurt than angry and he was the one who had broken the trust.

Alvin turned to leave.

"Wait. Leave the butter and eggs," Arthur said, and Alvin placed the parcel on the porch and left. As he turned toward his house, he saw Arthur pick up the parcel and retreat inside. He laughed to himself and looked up to see Mary in an upstairs window. She smiled and blew him a kiss. He pretended to catch it and put it in his shirt pocket, then blew her one back. Mary smiled and waved then disappeared from the window.

The next morning, he tried again and met with the same response. This time when she blew him a kiss from the window, he pretended to fumble it and drop it on the ground. He picked up the imaginary kiss and dusted it off, placing it in his shirt pocket again and patted it for safekeeping. Mary laughed and waved, then her smile disappeared, and Arthur was in the window. He scowled and pulled the curtains shut.

This went on for days. One morning, on his way down to their farm, Alvin found a collection of bluejay feathers on the side of the road, from where one was caught by another animal.

He collected the long feathers and each day after Arthur's re-buff, he would stick one into the bark of maple that sat at the front of their farm. Mary didn't appear in the window, but each day the previous day's feather was gone. It was her favorite bird, and the feathers were his signal to her that he loved her and was thinking of her.

St. Patrick's Day fell on a Wednesday, and Alvin made his daily trek to the McCalls. He was armed with two fresh soda breads, butter, eggs and a bottle of Irish whiskey he had paid far too much for in Monroe. It wasn't a common thing to get, so Parker Moreland helped him procure it from a man at the Monroe rail yard.

When he stepped onto the porch, he could smell a corned beef roast cooking. The smell of coriander filled the air, and his stomach growled.

Arthur opened the door and glared at Alvin. "My answer hasn't changed."

Alvin looked at Arthur with pathetic looking eyes. "For the love of God, Arthur. Can we call a truce for today? Forget the girl. I just want a bit of that roast. Not a lot. Just a taste."

Arthur stood for a moment frowning, then saw the bottle of Bushmills, and laughed. "Today. But tomorrow, we'll resume our hostilities."

"I can't ask for more than that," said Alvin. "Do have glass-es?"

Arthur pulled the bottle from the basket. "I'll find some."

Supper was tense. Alvin had to sit away from Mary, and any attempt at communication was interrupted by Arthur's need for butter or salt or anything that cut the conversation short. Alvin drank sparingly and made certain that Arthur had twice the whiskey he had. He ate sparingly as well and after the meal, he sat with Arthur next to the woodstove where the intense heat, full stomach and half bottle of whiskey finally took effect and Arthur fell asleep.

He went to the kitchen to see Mary, and Catherine met him in the doorway. "Where are you off to?"

"I want to talk to Mary."

Catherine paused and looked at Mary who was standing holding a dishcloth barely breathing in anticipation of the answer.

"I want her back in thirty minutes," she said, and Mary rushed to get her coat. "If he wakes and you're gone. You take the consequences on your own."

"We will", said Alvin and they left the house, closing the door quietly behind them.

They walked and held hands and when they were out of sight of the house, he kissed her and she squeezed him so tight, he wondered if he could ever pry her off. They caught up on everything that was going on and she pulled a bluejay feather from her pocket.

"Are these are from you?"

"They are."

"I never saw you place one. But I knew they were."

When they walked into the yard, they released their hands, and Alvin hated the feeling of distance that they'd need to endure.

"Why stop now." They heard a voice call and saw Arthur standing on the porch with his arms folded. "Wait til I'm napping and sneak off again."

"It's not like that." Alvin said in defiance.

"Oh really? How is it then?"

Alvin walked to the railing, and Arthur stood high on the porch. Alvin felt like he was pleading his case to a judge in court. "I love your daughter. I want to raise your grandchildren and we'll be married. That's the end of it. The longer you wait, the bigger her belly will get."

"Huh. I'll send her to a convent." Arthur scoffed.

"Well, I'll go get her. She's not a slave and she if marries Christ, she'll be divorcing him. I promise you that."

Arthur shook his head. "A fornicator and a blasphemer. What kind of an example would that be for my grandchild?"

Alvin knew he had him. If Arthur was talking about church, he had no more weapons left in his arsenal. "The best kind. The kind that loves her more than life itself and I'll risk going to hell if I have to so that I spend my time left here with her."

Arthur looked at them both then tilted his head and studied Alvin. "Oh God dammit...You have my blessing."

Mary squealed with delight and threw her arms around Alvin. He kissed her and smiled, then he looked to Arthur and nodded. Arthur nodded back. It was an acknowledgement of mutual respect.

Artur turned and opened the door, then called out. "Get in here and have a toast with me."

They went inside and Arthur poured drinks for Catherine, Alvin, and himself. He pointed to Mary. "You drink milk."

They picked up their drinks and Arthur looked at Alvin and Mary. "May your joys be deep as the ocean, and your troubles light as it's foam. May you find happiness, and love, in an ever-growing home. May you always have walls for the winds, a roof for the rain, and tea beside the fire. Laughter to cheer you, those you love near you, and all your heart's desire. Slainte."

Slainte, they repeated and drank the toast.

Five

M ary and Alvin were accompanied by her father into Monroe to speak with the new Parrish priest, Father Rancourt. He had only been in Monroe for a year, but people seemed to be taking to him. He was French Canadian and at first people were skeptical. They had only ever had an Irish priest until this one, but he had a quiet demeanor that the people liked. The previous priest, Father Dooley had a habit of becoming more and more animated as mass went on and his presence at weddings was usually a damped as he felt a need to lecture the wedding goers on the sins of excess of drink and lust during the reception.

Father Rancourt was a younger man with the soft, portly build that many priests had. He wore round glasses and had a receding hairline, even though he couldn't be much more than thirty. He sat quietly with his hands folded in his lap and listened as Alvin explained the situation. When Alvin was finished, father Rancourt unfolded his hands and tugged at his collar, which appeared to be too tight around his thick neck.

"I appreciate you coming to see me, and I can also appreciate your need for expediency. The problem is that the church will not allow me to marry you here without a special dispensation from the bishop."

"Is that hard to get?" asked Alvin.

Father Rancourt gave him a kindly smile. "Nearly impossible."

"We need to be married in the church, father. We want our baby to be baptized," said Mary.

The priest looked at the couple and nodded. "I believe I may have a solution. After all, you are not the first couple to conceive out of wedlock. Most people would just hide it from me and have a quick ceremony, and the miracle of a six-month pregnancy would occur after the wedding."

Arthur laughed aloud at that. "I've been to a few of those myself, father."

"What's your solution, father?" asked Alvin.

"I want you both to go to confession. Make a sincere act of contrition and do your penance. I still can't marry you here, but I will come to your home and perform the ceremony. Being married in a church is not what makes it binding in god's eyes, it's having a priest perform the ceremony."

Mary looked at the priest as he waited for their answer. "Will you get in trouble, father?"

The priest chuckled softly. "No. I won't get into trouble. I'll make a confession as well and will be absolved. No one would argue that having less Catholics is a good thing. I know of at least one more that will be coming later this year and I expect, for years to come."

Alvin looked at Mary, and she nodded. He turned back to the priest. "Thank you, father. We accept your conditions. When would be convenient for you to perform the ceremony?"

Father Rancourt thought for a moment. "Well, Easter is on the eleventh of April and Palm Sunday on the fourth. I don't do weddings in the church on those weekends, so pick the Saturday before either of those, and I'll come to you."

Alvin turned to Mary. "Do you have a preference?"

"Can we do the tenth?"

"Of course. But do you want to wait that long?" asked Alvin.

She smiled. "I don't, but won't your friend Richard be here by then?"

Alvin was so caught up in the whirlwind since Arthur blessed the union that he has forgotten that Richard was coming. "He is. The tenth would be grand."

"Excellent. Let's move over to the church and hear your confessions and that will be out of the way."

They each took a turn in the confessional and each left with their own penance to say a rosary every day until the wedding and they both agreed that it was a small price to pay to avoid a civil ceremony.

True to the saying, March had come in like a lion and left like a lamb. The mild weather at the end of march has spilled into April which had been sunny most days and unseasonably warm. The snows receded, except in the woods where pockets of crystal ice still clung to their places in the shade.

Arthur had let Mary return to Alvin's farm whenever her chores were done at home, and she busied herself cleaning the flowerbeds of debris where she and Alvin had planted bulbs the previous year. She kneeled in the mud on a folded piece of canvas. It worked for a little while before the moisture soaked through, but she didn't care.

In her dreams, she would always have a house with beautiful flower beds to bring the butterflies and bees to the yard. She had always liked the old Hartley farm with its wrap-around porch and big maple tree in the yard. In many ways, it looked like her father's farm, but the Hartley's always had more color. Apple trees and magnolias were scattered around the property near the house, and they were in perpetual bloom throughout the spring. The McCall farm had a few maples, which supplied them with sap for making syrup, but it lacked the flare of the Hartley place. She certainly never thought she would be living less than a mile from her home. She had always imagined she'd be at a house near town, with neighbors to each side that she might chat with while hanging laundry or taking her children to the market.

Mary finished weeding the first bed and stood to look at it. Her crocus, tulips and daffodils were all in various states of bloom. She'd have to wait another month or so for her irises. Those were her favorite, except, of course, for her sunflowers. She planted both short and tall sunflowers and she was waiting until the last frost to start them, but that might not be until May. Mary was always careful to collect as many seeds as she could from her plants. This was the tenth generation of mammoth sunflowers from the one she had grown for her mother when she started school. It was a single seed in a clay pot to teach children about plants, and every year she collected the seeds and planted more and more. She knew that she had planted more than a hundred sunflowers from that original plant.

She brought her basket of weeds to throw onto the manure pile and saw Alvin emerge from the barn with sawdust and shavings on his clothes.

"What are you about in there?" she asked.

Alvin grinned and shook his head. "A surprise. But don't go in the wood shop. I don't want to see it until I'm done."

Mary dumped the weeds and walked toward him. She leaned forward and kissed him on the cheek. "I won't. I like surprises."

Alvin wrapped his arm around her and hugged her tight. "I need to clean up before we go to get Richard. I'm going to put some water on to heat so I don't freeze cleaning up."

"I'll come in and wash your back for you."

Alvin smiled. "Mmmm. I'd like that."

Mary pulled away and looked into his eyes. "I'll wash your back...and nothing more. We're waiting now."

Alvin scrunched his face and scratched his head. He looked down at her belly. "A bit late for that isn't it?"

"I don't care. And I'm not showing yet... If you can't behave yourself, you can wash your own back."

Alvin smiled and took her by the hand. "I'll behave... and we'll wait. I just don't want to pick Richard up smelling of cow shit."

"Well, wear clean boots then. I could smell you ten feet away." She thought for a moment and smelled herself. "Actually, I think I'll wash as well. Will you do my back?"

"Happily."

They walked to the house and heard the loud song of a cardinal. Alvin turned to the lilac and there on a branch was a large male. "They're a beautiful bird. I'm not sure which I like more the bluejays or the cardinals."

Mary watched it calling out searching the sky for a mate. "They say that when cardinals appear, an angel is near."

Alvin chuckled. "In Ireland, it's bad luck to kill a robin, because people believe that they carry the spirits of dead loved ones."

Mary took his hand, and they stepped onto the porch. " I hope it's true. Everyone would be safer with an angel around."

"We don't need an angel. We have each other." He leaned over and kissed her cheek. "But then again. You can never be too careful."

Mary stood beside Alvin as they waited for the evening train to arrive. She hadn't seen him this nervous since he had to tell her father he had made her pregnant. Alvin paced and checked his watch.

"It's only four fifty, and the train isn't due until five," she said. "Trains are very punctual you know."

Alvin blushed and laughed. "I don't know why I'm so nervous. He's very jovial and I'm sure he's going to be happy to be here."

Mary took his hand. "You miss your friend and you're eager to see him. It's understandable to be excited."

Alvin kissed her cheek. "You are right, of course. He's a good man and he's been good to me. I can't wait to introduce you."

Mary's smile disappeared. "I'm anxious to meet him too. I hope he likes me as much as Edna. It sounded like he loved her."

Alvin stroked her cheek with is hand. "He'll love you too. Richard is a very large man, but it's mostly heart."

Mary smiled and saw smoke rising from the south over Alvin's shoulder and pointed. "I think they might be a few minutes early."

Alvin turned to see the train's smoke rising over the trees and heard the call of the whistle as it made its last turn into the station.

Six

Alvin watched as the passengers disembarked from the evening train. He watched in the windows to see if a massive man was making his way forward, but he saw none. His heart sank, and he started to move down the line, looking into all the windows. When he reached the end looked to see if anyone had gotten off the further down the line but saw nothing but freight cars.

"What are you looking for!" he heard a man call out and saw a large young man with red hair. He looked like Richard, but much smaller in girth.

Alvin studied the man and smiled. It was Richard, and he has lost a tremendous amount of weight. Alvin walked to him and extended, "M'lord."

Richard laughed and threw his arms around Alvin. "For Christ's sake, man. Just Richard. I hold no titles here."

Alvin laughed. "I'm sorry. I didn't recognize you. I think you left half of you back in England."

Richard stood tall and turned his head to both sides. "I left ten stone there. Twenty, if you include my wife," he said with a booming laugh. "My God, it's good to see you McGinn."

"The weight? How did you..."

Richard shook his head. "Necessity caused me to lose the weight."

Alvin gave him a puzzled look. "I don't understand."

"I was sitting down to a dinner in London at a friend's home and when I sat in the chair, it collapsed under my enormous ass. It was London society, so everyone feigned politeness, but Eliza-Mae was mortified, of course, and honestly, so was I."

"I'm sorry that happened," Alvin said and felt sorrow for his friend.

"I'm not. I think when you reach that size, you think that there is no way back. But I endeavored to live a healthier life and to be quite frank, I was in a pitiful state. No wonder my wife never wanted me."

Alvin smiled. "Is she happy now?"

Richard laughed. "Oh God no. She still loathes me, but I do hold out hope that she might come around and we might conceive a child someday."

Alvin placed his hand on Richard's shoulder. "I want that for you above all things."

Richard smiled and hugged Alvin again. "It's good to see you my friend."

Alvin looked to his left and saw Mary standing with her hands clasped in front of her. She had a look of pure joy at seeing the friends reunited. He turned Richard's body to meet her. "Richard. This is my wife to be. Miss Mary McCall."

Richard stood tall once again and stepped forward, taking Mary's hand and kissing the back of it. "Enchante," he said and studied her face. "McGinn. I am both delighted and envious of you. It must be that damned stone of yours. You're not pretty enough to have a young lady like this."

Mary blushed and grinned. "I'm so pleased to meet you, Lord Ellingwood. Alvin has talked about you so much I feel that I know you already."

Richard smiled. "Mary, please call me Richard. Alvin is a dear friend, and my heart overflows with joy for you both."

Mary smiled and nodded. "Thank you...Richard, and you are right. I'm powerless to his charms."

Alvin rolled his eyes and shook his head. "We should get to the farm before it's dark."

Richard took Mary by the arm. "Please lead the way and regale me with how my friend captured the heart of such a beautiful woman."

They brought Mary to the McCall farm first. Alvin had expected to visit briefly and leave, returning tomorrow to have a proper visit, but Arthur met them at the porch and insisted they stay for at least one drink. That turned into two. Which led to a fire and the cracking of a bottle of the Moreland's Canadian whiskey.

It was well beyond dark, and Richard and Alvin were well beyond drunk by the time they headed back to his farm.

"Since I lost the weight, I can't drink like I used to," Richard said and shook his head, trying to clear his vision.

Alvin had lanterns on the wagon, and fortunately it was a straight road between the two farms. Pal and Chum had made the trip so many times, he barely needed to steer them. When they arrived, Alvin unharnessed the horses and led them into their stalls. He did it so briskly that Richard just watched in awe.

"You're a proper farmer McGinn."

Alvin laughed. "Middling at best. But thanks."

Richard walked over and patted Buddy's head through the wooden door that let Alvin feed him. "I like horses. You know the thing that bothered me the most about being so fat?"

Alvin looked at him and shook his head, "you're too hard on yourself."

"It was being too fat to hunt that bothered me the most. I loved a good fox hunt as a young man, but the fatter I got, the slower my horses were, and I struggled to keep up." He stroked Buddy's soft nose. "I know it embarrassed my father, so I made excuses not to go out with him and my brothers, to the point that they stopped inviting me."

"Well, you can certainly go now," said Alvin with a tone of encouragement.

Richard nuzzled his forehead against Buddy's face and patted him on the head. "No one invites me anymore."

Alvin looked at his old friend and could see the pain on his face. "Tomorrow's another day. A new day. Anything is possible."

The first rays of the morning sun brought the rooster's annoying call. Alvin crammed a pillow over his head and tried to go back to sleep. By the third call, he realized that he was late for milking and sat up quickly. The whiskey still swam in his head, and he felt his stomach churn in defiance of rising.

"Bloody hell," he whispered in a loud exhale. He went to the sink and worked the pump until water poured onto the slate. Alvin laid his head under the flow and let the water pour over his face.

"Does it help?" he heard Richard ask.

Alvin stood up and shook the water from his hair. "Brrrr. Not really. But I have to tend the animals."

Richard looked around the kitchen. "This place is more impressive than the cottage."

Alvin nodded and smiled. "It is. But Christ it takes a lot to heat it in the winter and I kept the upstairs closed."

"There seems to be plenty of wood around. I can't see anything through the trees," Richard said with a laugh.

Alvin smoothed his wet hair back and added opened the kitchen stove. A few embers remained, but not enough to just throw some new wood on. He grabbed a handful of cedar sticks from his kindling basket and laid them on the coals. The wood smoked and snapped and soon caught flame. Sparks rose and crackled in the stove, and he added some small sticks of ash, then replaced the cover. "Coffee or tea?"

Richard watched in amazement at the ease with which Alvin restored the flames. "Tea if you have it."

Alvin filled the pot with water and slid it over the burner. "It'll be a minute."

Richard watched his friend moving about the kitchen, preparing to make the tea. "She's an amazing girl you know."

"Mary?"

Richard frowned. "Of course, Mary. Who else would I be talking about... She reminds me of Edna. Not in looks, but in spirit."

Alvin laughed to himself. "I see it too... Sometimes I wonder how I could get so lucky to find two women like that in one lifetime."

Richard pulled a white pipe with a black stem from his pocket and loaded it. He picked up the box of matches from the table and lit it. He looked at Alvin and waved the match to extinguish it, then tossed it into the ashtray. "They are out there. I'm convinced of it. The challenge is finding the one that's right for you."

"That's easier said than done. That's why I feel so lucky to have found two."

Richard puffed the pipe and blew smoke into the air. "It is luck when you think of it. Most men marry women they know and see, and women have an even smaller choice. Most of them are limited to what men stay in the town they are born. If it's a city like London, there are plenty of choices. But out here? If you hadn't come here, what choices would she have had?"

Alvin shrugged. "Few. I supposed there are plenty of men in town. But out here, not so much."

Richard puffed and studied Alvin. "I can see she makes you happy, and it's clear that she adores you. Do you love her as much as Edna?"

Alvin smiled. "I do."

"Do you love her more than yourself?"

It was an odd question, and Alvin tried to make sense of it, but he felt like he knew where Richard was going. "I do. I treasure her above all things."

Richard smiled. "Good. I think that is the biggest problem with Eliza-Mae. We never had that feeling that the other's life was more important than our own. How I envy you. Twice in one lifetime and for me, despite my wealth, I'll never know that feeling."

Alvin could see his friend becoming melancholy. "You don't know that. You could have a child and that could change her perspective."

45

Richard laughed aloud. "Oh, I am sure it would. Then she'd be able to chastise me for giving her a child that disrupted her sleep. A new perspective indeed."

Seven

Mary enjoyed the way Alvin lit up around Richard. He was proud to introduce everyone to his friend and proud to introduce everyone to Richard. No one had ever met nobility before, even if it was from another country. Even her father liked him and that was saying a lot, considering that Richard was English.

Alvin wanted Richard to meet the Morelands, so they all rode together in the buckboard over to see the Major. Mary sat on the bench between them. Alvin with his long lanky frame and Richard with his broad chest and shoulders. They talked about people she had never met, which felt awkward, but the stories were funny enough that she just imagined who the people were.

The funniest story was about his wife arguing with her sister about the best way to feed swans and falling into the pond while she demonstrated her technique. She could only imagine the people, but she had gleaned that she was attractive, but with large teeth and was usually very judgmental. Richard had used the term, looking down her pointed nose at people, more than a few times.

Alvin had told Mary of the Manor house on Richard's estate, and she wondered how it compared to the Moreland house. It was a large Georgian style house with a portico in the front supported by massive columns. The house was completely white, except for black shutters and even the chimneys were painted white with a black band at the top. Her father had explained that before the Revolutionary war, it was a symbol to show you were a loyalist. During the civil war, it was a sign that it was a safe place for runaway slaves. But in Moreland's case, the house was built after both, so her father told her it was just a way to hide the soot stains on his otherwise pristine house.

They could see major Moreland standing on the front steps, dressed in a dark suit with a royal blue vest. It was the same color as the blue in the Scottish flag. Moreland stood proudly and smiled as the wagon approached.

Alvin pulled in under the portico and locked the brake so that they could disembark the torturous bench. *Alvin needs to pad that bench someday*, Mary thought as she tried to rub some feeling back into her buttocks. She wiped her hands on her skirt to make it seem like she was flattening her clothes. After all, who wants to kiss hand of a woman who'd been massaging her backside just a moment before.

Alvin dismounted and helped Mary down then stood up straight and stepped forward to the smiling Major. "Major.

Thank you for having us." He turned to Mary, I believe you know my bride to be. Miss Mary McCall."

Morland smiled and kissed the back of Mary's hand. "Of course I do. She used to accompany her father to the horse races. I think his wife sent the girl to keep Arthur out of mischief," he said with a laugh.

"Did it ever work?" Mary asked.

"Hardly," replied Moreland with a grin.

Richard had made his way around the wagon and stood beside Alvin. They were of a similar height. Both were around six feet tall, but Richard looked like he could have made two Alvins.

Alvin stood proudly. "Major. I'd like you to meet my particular friend, Lord Richard Ellingwood."

Richard blushed. "Please Major, just call me Richard. I hold no titles or land here."

Moreland smiled and shook his hand with great vigor. "I am pleased to me you Richard. When Alvin told me your name, I couldn't wait to ask. Are you related to a General Ellingwood? Artillery commander. Charles, I think his name was."

Richard nodded. "I am sir. He was my father's brother."

Moreland's smile disappeared, "was?"

"Yes sir. I am afraid so. He was killed in 1900 in South Africa during the Boer war."

"Killed in action?" asked Moreland.

"Yes, sir."

"I'm sorry for it. I met him on two occasions and found him to be a true gentleman and a pleasant dinner companion."

Richard smiled. "I appreciate that. He was always kindly to me. Although he referred to me as that fat boy, I know he wasn't being cruel. It was a fact. I was a very fat boy," he said with a laugh.

"Well, you look fine now, sir." Moreland said. "Won't you come in? Young McGinn tells me you own a number of properties, I dabbed in land myself, you know."

Richard smiled. "A sound investment. God won't be making anymore of it."

Moreland laughed a loud. "Quite right. That's very witty. I think I'll use that line myself. Won't you all come inside. My wife is quite eager to meet you."

***

Mary stepped into the large foyer with eyes wide. She had never been in a house so large in her life and she tried to imagine cleaning a house this size. The ceilings seemed to be twice as high as the ceilings at the farm. Her best guess was fourteen feet. The entry had a staircase to the right and benches to the left. Her ears were drawn to the methodical ticking of a grandfather clock. Like everything else in the house, it was intimidating, too. The clock must have been close to eight feet tall with a face that must have been two feet across.

Elizabeth Moreland stood waiting in a royal blue dress gathered by an ivory-colored sash. Her brown hair was done up nicely in a neat bun and Mary thought that she may be the most elegant lady she had ever met.

Elizabeth stepped forward to Richard and smiled. "Lord Ellingwood, it is a pleasure to meet you."

Richard bowed and kissed the back of her hand. Mary had never seen anything like that. She had heard of it of course, but the McCalls were huggers. Most people weren't eager to kiss the hands of farm girls with their callouses and cracked skin from years of hard work. Still, she found it pleasing that courtesy was paramount in the upper class, even if it was mostly for appearances.

When she finished with the gentlemen, she made her way to Mary. "Miss McCall, you look positively radiant."

"Thank you, Mam. That may be the most beautiful dress I have ever seen. What is it made from. It has a wonderful shine."

"It's taffeta, my dear." She leaned in as if to share a secret and whispered. "I like the shine, but I'm afraid it's prone to wrinkling. That's why ladies look so stiff at formal events."

"I see," said Mary, trying to think if she had ever seen a formal event.

"That, and they do tend to be stuck up. Most society parties end up being an ostentation of peacocks, each trying to outdo the others."

Mary's eyes widened. "I doubt I'll ever be invited to society events unless it's a grange outing."

Elizabeth laughed. "I suspect it's much the same there, just the clothing is probably less expensive."

Mary laughed at that. "It is. It seems that they all want to fight over the same men."

"You see. It's the same everywhere. Would you like to join me in the salon while the men speak with Malcolm?"

Mary smiled and nodded. She had no idea what a salon was but followed along so as not to look lost.

Elizabeth led her into a room to the right of the staircase. It had a large fireplace at one and a serving buffet, with tea and cakes to the left. The room was ornate with paintings and large plants that Mary had never seen in Maine. "Would you care for some music?" asked Elizabeth.

Mary blushed, "I'm sorry Mrs. Moreland. I don't play an instrument."

Elizabeth grinned but held back from laughing. "Neither do I. But we do have a phonograph. It's quite a miraculous invention."

"I've heard of them, but I've never actually seen one."

"Well, this will be a treat, then." Elizabeth opened a wooden case, revealing a disc, and cranked a handle on the side. She flipped a small lever, and the disc began to spin, and she dropped a round device with a needle onto the disc.

At first, Mary only heard crackling, then the soft, deep sound of a cello followed four beats later by a violin. She stood in awe that music could travel from that disc through a needle to become music. She had heard about phonographs, but no one that she knew had enough money to own one. Most of the families she knew made their own music. They all played the same Irish jigs and drinking songs. They played them on fiddles, spoons, bodhrán drums and whatever else people could make music with. "It's beautiful." Mary said aloud.

Elizabeth took her by both hands. "I said the same thing the first time I heard one, and it's much less disruptive than having live musicians, having to frequently stop conversations because someone decided a certain piece required applause. They are professional musicians. It's their job. But can you imagine if when you went to the bank and the teller gave you correct change everyone stopped to applaud them doing their job. It would take all day to make a deposit."

Mary blushed and looked at the floor. "I've never been to a bank."

Elizabeth paused and smiled. "I'm certain you will someday. Anyway, my point is that the phonograph doesn't require applause. Just a frequent crank and a decent selection of discs. Let's sit and talk about your wedding. I love weddings. It's a day when the bride is the center of everyone's attention. We don't get many days like that."

Eight

The sun crested Howell Hill like a curious child peeking around a doorway to see what was happening in the valley. Alvin and Richard sat on the porch drinking tea in the cool morning air. It was early April, and the frost still clung to the grass, making it look more silver than green. Richard sat reclined with his eyes closed, feeling the sunlight warm his face, while Alvin gripped his tea, trying to steady his nerves.

It was his wedding day, and his mind raced from thoughts of the new baby, back to Edna and Nora. In his heart, he loved Mary as much as he had ever loved anyone, even so, he couldn't shake Edna from his mind. Maybe he wasn't supposed to. He had seen lots of robins here, but none that followed him or sat and watched him. He fought to reconcile his mind that this is what she would have wanted. Simply for him to be happy.

His thoughts were pierced by the sharp song of a cardinal. He looked to the lilac tree but didn't see any. He heard the song again and searched the trees. When he didn't find any he started to whistle to mimic the song.

Richard groaned. "Christ, old boy. Do you have to do that so early? My head is pounding from your father-in-law's vile liquor."

Alvin ignored him and called again. "It's nearby now," he said in a whisper, and searched the skies. The song was louder, so Alvin repeated the call loudly again. "It's right here. I just can't find it." On his next attempt, a blur of red swooped down from the roof and fluttered in his face. Alvin jumped and spilled the hot tea on himself and dropped his cup. The tin cup clanged on the porch splashing tea on his shoes. At the sound of the clang, the cardinal disappeared as quickly as it had come.

Richard roared with laughter. "I don't know who was startled more. You or the bird!"

Alvin shook his head and kicked the tea from his feet. "Well, the bird doesn't have wet feet."

Richard smiled and looked at his friend. "Wet feet will dry. Cold feet, now that's another story. Are you nervous?"

Alvin picked up the cup and sat in his chair, then lit his pipe. "I am. But not the way you might think."

"What do you mean?"

"I'm not nervous to get married. I just worry that I'm somehow insulting Edna's memory. Perhaps it was too soon."

Richard inhaled deeply and sighed. "You're fine. Edna would be pleased. Mary is a fine young woman, and I see Edna in her. Not in looks, though God knows they are both beautiful and

I don't know what they saw in you." Richard chuckled and sipped his tea. "It's their spirits that are similar. They're both strong, but delicate. They are kind and content. Believe me, that is a trait that I haven't had the pleasure of seeing."

"Did you know that Mary has made all of my shirts since arriving?"

Richard looked at Alvin's flannel work shirt and searched for imperfections. "That shirt you're wearing now?"

Alvin looked at the shirt. "Yes. She made it."

"My God. She's a prodigious talent with a needle and thread."

Alvin laughed. "If you're impressed by that, you should come back at the end of the summer and see this garden. It looks like something from the great estates in Ireland. We grow enough food to last the full winter. It's her. I till the soil and plant where she tells me. She understands it all far beyond my comprehension."

Richard stood and placed his hand on Alvin's shoulder. "I wish you could have seen your face just now, when you talked of Mary. It's the face of a man who loves a woman. Edna's been gone a long time now. Keep her in your heart, but it's time to move on now."

Alvin heard what he was saying and felt in his heart that it was the truth. "Mary's pregnant you know."

Richard raised his eyebrows but betrayed no other emotion. "I'm happy for you, my friend."

Albin smiled. "I thought Arthur might shoot me when I told him, but he came around after a bit of threats and torment."

Richard looked at the size of the farmhouse. "You'll have space for this one and plenty more."

"Two will probably be plenty. A boy and a girl are what she wants."

"I'm proud of you, brother. You've made a fine life for yourself here. I wish you all the happiness in the world."

Alvin nodded and smiled. "Thank you. I always appreciate your counsel." Alvin picked up his cup. "I have some of Moreland's Canadian Whiskey. I'll make us some coffee and put a drop of whiskey in it to clear our heads."

"Hang the coffee." Richard flung the rest of his tea into the yard, "just grab the bottle."

Mary stood looking into a mirror as Catherine made the final adjustments to her dress. The dress was the same one she had worn when she married Arthur. She had added some pearl adornments to make it more elegant, but when she stood beside Mary and looked into the mirror, she could she herself on her wedding day.

"I hope you enjoy all the love and happiness that I have with your father. I couldn't have asked for a better life."

Mary smiled and her eyes started to well up. "I wish... I wouldn't have..."

"Shhh, hush child. There's no crying now. You'll foul your face powder." She handed Mary a silk handkerchief. "Dab it. Don't swipe at it."

Mary carefully dabbed her eyes. "Thank you."

"I don't judge you. God knows how young people are. The virgin Mary was pregnant before she was married. She moved about five towns away to have Jesus you know."

"But that was an angel that got her with child."

Catherine huffed. "Really? Back then, if you were found to be knocked up, they'd stone you in the town square. But if you said that God was the father, people might think twice before throwing a rock between your eyes." Catherine looked at Mary's stunned face and winked.

Mary laughed and shook her head. "You better not let Father Rancourt hear you talking like that. I have callouses on my fingertips from saying all those rosaries as penance."

"Bah. I've said plenty of rosaries. What's a few more."

Their conversation was interrupted by a commotion outside, and Mary headed to the window.

Catherine shouted, "Stop!"

Mary jumped and turned. "What?"

"I'll look. If you see the groom before you're married, it's bad luck. ". Catherine moved to the window and peeked out from between the curtains. It was Alvin and Richard arriving by carriage, along with the Major and his wife.

"I saved you there. It's him."

Mary fought back the urge to look and asked, "How does he look?"

"Like the luckiest man on earth."

Arthur stood at the door, waiting for Mary. The family was assembled and Alvin stood with the priest. He folded his hands to look calm, but every few seconds he wiped them on his coat to dry his sweaty palms. Behind them were two kneelers that Arthur had made for the ceremony. The young priest had made an exception for the guest to remain seated, but insisted that Alvin and Mary kneel like proper Catholics.

When Mary arrived at the doorway, Arthur gasped and fought back tears. He could feel his face flush and he smiled, then wiped his eyes. "Pollen."

Mary laughed. "Please don't do that. You'll make me cry and spoil my cosmetics."

"You're a vision. Pure and simple. I can't believe I had a hand in making anything so lovely." Arthur turned and offered his elbow to her. The sound of a fiddle filled the air and Arthur smiled. The song was My Wild Irish Rose. It was the same song they played when he married Catherine. The sound touched him deep in his heart and this time there was no holding back the tears. He didn't care. If a father couldn't cry at his own daughter's wedding, there was something wrong with the world, not him. As he approached Alvin, he took Mary's hand and offered it to him. "Take care of my girl..." He seemed like he was about to say something else, but wiped his eyes before turning. "Pollen."

Alvin grinned and nodded. "Thank you, Arthur."

Father Rancourt started the service with a welcome and a reading. He had Mary and Alvin kneel through much of the ceremony, and Alvin's eyes were drawn to a pair of tan cardinals flitting from limb to limb in an apple tree that stood a few yards away. They seemed to be playing, and both took turns singing their cardinal songs.

When at last he could kiss Mary again, he lifted her veil and felt his heart melt in his chest. She was stunning, and no longer looked much like a girl. She was a young woman. He leaned in and kissed her lips to howls, cheers and whistles. He took her hand and turned to face their family and friends, with as much pride as any man alive. When the cheering stopped, they walked together into the group and received their congratulations. He looked back at the apple tree to see that the two cardinals had gone. *Probably all the commotion*, he thought, or *maybe they've flown back to heaven.*

Nine

After the wedding, Richard stayed another week before returning to England. He promised Alvin that he would look in on his family when he returned to Ireland for the summer and that he would be back in a year or two. April turned to May, and the flowers were in full bloom when Mary started planting their garden. Alvin prepared the garden spot, but Mary insisted on doing the planting herself. There was something about having her hands in the soil that made her feel good.

She thought about the seed sprouting and growing into a plant, flowering and then producing a vegetable or fruit. She felt a kinship with the soil, because soon she would bear a child and by the time these plants were ready to harvest, the baby would be here as well.

Alvin hovered constantly and made several trips a day from whatever he was doing to make certain she was okay. He even went as far as to take her to Monroe to meet with a physician to make sure everything was okay. Doctor Turner gave her a clean bill of health and that went a long way to settle Alvin's fears, but he hovered all the same.

When she finished planting, she went to the barn to wash before milking. Alvin had taken Buddy and Pal to the woods, giving Chum a day off. The gray pony stood at the gate between the corral and the barn, watching her wash. She turned to pick up the milk pail, and he gave a loud puff that made his lips rumble.

"What are you griping about young man? You've been relaxing all day."

Chum stomped his hoof and puffed again.

"You want a drink? There's a trough right over there." She said and pointed to the large tin tub that served as the animal's watering station.

Chum stomped and whinnied.

Mary opened the apple barrel from the fall and grabbed two large Macs. Macintosh was the most popular apple in central Maine, and the property had six trees planted near the back wood line, so that's what they had the most of. Unfortunately, they had been in the barrel so long, they weren't really very good for eating anymore, but the animals enjoyed them greatly.

Alvin had warned Mary never to trust Chum, but she felt bad for him and crept over to him with an apple in each hand. "It's the bottom of the barrel, but don't tell Alvin I gave you an apple. He'll be cross with me. He's worried we'll run out of apples for pie."

As she approached, Chum stomped and became more agitated, puffing impatiently.

"Stop that foolishness or you'll get nothing." She held an apple out at arms lengths and Chum lurched forward and snapped it in half. She stood looking at the half she was still holding, wondering if he had gotten a finger. All of her digits were intact, and he bobbed his head up and down. "Easy this time." She held the half-eaten apple in her palm and, as if he could sense that he had been too aggressive, he gently wrapped his mouth around the rest and chomped it slowly. Mary moved closer and stroked his muzzle. She offered the second apple, and he took the whole thing into his mouth and chewed it in silence. When she touched his face again, he pressed into her, and she scratched his face.

Chum tilted his head and pressed it hard against her. Mary smiled. "You are such a man. The path to your heart is through your stomach."

She hadn't noticed Alvin returning from the woods and was startled when she heard him bring the team into the front of the barn. Chum stomped and jumped back. The quick movement made her step back quickly, and she tripped on the milk pail, falling to the floor with a thud.

Before she had realized what had happened, Alvin was at her side in a panic. "Did he bite you?!"

"No. nothing of the sort. We were just becoming friends, and you startled us. That's all."

Alvin looked at Chum who was still standing in the doorway. He stood defiant with his ears laid back. "Friends? With that little bastard. Look at him. He'd like to bite me right now."

Mary shook her head and reached out. Alvin took her by the arm and helped her to her feet. "He's a man. He likes women. Maybe you should try a gentler approach."

"Bah. If it's a war of wills, I will win."

Mary shook her head. "He's jealous of you. That's all."

"He's a little bastard, is what he is. But are you hurt anywhere?"

Mary rubbed her bottom. "Just my backside. You can rub it later if you'd like."

"Whatever you think would help."

Mary laughed. "I don't know if it would help, but I know you like to rub it, so that'll be your chance."

Mary sat sewing squares for a quilt while Alvin read at the table. She admired him in so many ways. He was naïve about some things, but he had a thirst for knowledge and could talk intelligently about most topics. History was his favorite, and he even impressed Major Moreland with his knowledge of the American wars.

Not long after the wedding, on a trip into Monroe led to a stop at Smith's Books and the purchase of a history book about of the United States. Alvin read it in a week and re-read it the following week. For the next month, Mary felt like she was back in school with a new history lesson every night.

"What are you reading tonight, love?"

Alvin lowered the book and smiled. "Hero tales from American history."

"Is it good?"

Alvin nodded and picked up his pipe. "It is. It covers generals and other military figures from Washinton to Lincoln."

"They told us in school that when Washington was a child, he chopped down a cherry tree and when his father asked who had done it. He said I cannot tell a lie, it was me."

"I hate to disappoint you darling. But this book says the story of the cherry tree was made up."

Mary's mouth dropped opened. "That's terrible. We were afraid of telling lies, because if George Washington didn't lie, then we shouldn't have. Would saved me from a switch a time or two if I had kept my lips shut."

Alvin laughed. "There's a bit of irony for you. The story about *not lying* is a lie itself."

"It's dishonest is what that is. Pure trickery."

Alvin puffed his pipe and blew it into the air. "Well, who's to say these fellas are right. You can't trust everything you read. Or hear for that matter."

Mary smiled and picked up her sewing. "Do you think they're right?"

"I'd never swear to it. The fellas that wrote it were politicians. You can't believe a bloody word they say."

Mary laughed. "My word. It sounds like I married my father."

Alvin returned to his book and Mary tried to sew but she was distracted watching him. She was proud to be his wife and knew that he'd be a wonderful father. She rose from the chair and took the pipe from his hand. He looked up and Mary took a puff and squinted. She exhaled and smiled at him with watery eyes. "Wew. Made me light-headed."

"It takes some practice to be sure."

She handed him his pipe and leaned in and kissed him. "I'm going to wash and go to bed. Sitting in that chair is making my backside feel worse."

Alvin tapped his pipe in the ashtray, laid a ribbon in his page as a bookmark and closed it. "I'll be up to rub it for you in a few minutes"

"Rub it whenever you want, so long as it get's rubbed."

Alvin placed the book on the table and hopped to his feet. "Actually, I think I'll come now."

The sun felt good on Mary's face as she and Alvin enjoyed their morning coffee on the porch. It had become their morning routine as soon as April turned to May. She cherished these moments of peace. They both worked hard and once the day began, there was little respite until the sun began to set. The air was filled with bird songs and the buzzing of insects. After the long Maine winters, she always appreciated the sounds of nature. Winter had a stillness to it, except for the howling of the north winds. But spring brought everything back to life.

The morning air was split be the piercing call of a Cardinal. "Oh, your friend is back," she said with a light laugh.

"He's fond of hide and seek," replied Alvin. "You'd think being red, they'd be easy to spot."

Mary stood up and looked down the road. "I see something red."

"A cardinal?"

Mary stepped to the edge of the porch and whistled.

Alvin looked up to see Arthur walking in the road and Toto running straight toward the farm walk.

Alvin shrugged. "Oh," he said in a dispassionate tone.

Mary frowned. "Don't be cruel. I miss my dog." She walked down the steps and Toto jumped about her in a whirl of red hair. "There's my beautiful boy!" She kneeled down and hugged him around his long neck.

"At least it's an Irish dog."

Mary shook her head. "It shouldn't matter if he's from Timbuktu. He's my dog and you should love him as much as me."

Alvin sat silent for a moment, trying to come up with something witty to say. As he was about to give up, he smiled. "Mary, I could never love anything as much as I love you."

Ten

The morning dew hung heavy on the grass as the sun crested Howell Hill making the yard look more silver than green. Alvin sat on the porch drinking coffee and reading his history book. As he raised the cup to his mouth, he saw a flash of auburn hair moving through the field. He heard a loud shriek of a whistle and Arthur walked into the yard with a wicker basket in one hand and a gallon jug in the other. "Morning, Arthur. What have you there?"

Arthur raised the basket in a half-hearted wave. "It's not the poteen, if that's what you're thinking. It's maple syrup the boys made."

Alvin scratched his head. "What are you doing with it?"

Arthur tilted his head and frowned. "I'm bringing it to you, along with this damned dog."

Alvin put his coffee cup down. "We don't need a dog."

Mary turned and scowled. "Alvin. That's not nice. I miss him...Here Toto!" The setter ran at a full sprint and jumped wildly until Mary could grab him enough to settle him down. The setter's tail wagged like a blur, and he licked Mary's face all over.

Arthur placed the basket and jug on the porch with a thud. "Christ, that's heavy when you carry it for a mile." He flexed his fingers and shook his head. "I planned on keeping the dog. He's a prime hunter, and I thought he and I were friends, but ever since she left," he said with a jerk of the thumb toward Mary, "all he does is mope around the farm and look out the window half a hundred times a day...It's a pitiful sight."

Alvin surveyed the dog and scratched at his own face stubble. "I don't imagine it would make any difference to protest?"

Mary stood and brushed herself off. "It wouldn't... Daddy, would you like some coffee?"

"I'd love some, my dear."

"I'll bring the pot," she said and stepped into the house with Toto hot on her heels.

Arthur pulled his pipe from his pocket and packed it with tobacco. "I might have a bit of work for you."

"I have enough work here most days, but what's afoot?"

Arthur lit his pipe and waved the spent match in the air, then tossed it on the ground. "I ran into Cy Hartley at Hemmings and he mentioned he's in the market for some pine and some cedar. He's mending his barn roof. He'll haul it and have it sawed up. All you have to do is get it out of the woods."

Alvin thought for a moment and nodded. "Seems fair enough. I'll stop in and see him next time I ride by."

"How's married life treating you?"

Alvin smiled and shook his head. "It's like a dream. I never thought I'd be able to love someone again, but I love your daughter completely. She has a strength that I admire very much."

Arthur watched his son-in-law as he professed his love and could see that he meant every word that left his lips. "You're a good lad... I could have wished you had waited, but the heart wants what it wants, I guess, and I wouldn't want anyone else for my Mary."

Alvin placed his hand on Arthur's shoulder. "Thank you, Arthur. That means more than you could ever know."

Alvin made his monthly trip to Hemmings for a couple of sacks of grain. He selected Chum and Pal to pull the wagon since Buddy and Chum still were prone to quarreling. When he pulled up to the Hartley farm, Cy and his wife, Julia were weeding their garden. Hartley stood and waved when he saw Alvin approach. "Art told you I wanted to see you?"

Alvin stopped the team and locked the brake. He jumped down shook Cy's hand. "Yes, he did. He said you were repairing a roof?"

Cy Hartley was a man in his early thirties with thinning hair and leathery tanned skin. He had salt and pepper hair and blue eyes that contrasted with his dark complexion. "I am. I had a pine topple onto it when we had that ice storm this past winter, and I need to replace some boards and shingles before I can put hay in there again."

"I've had a bit of experience with that myself. If you want a hand, let me know. I had a whole gang of farmers help me, seems the least I could do to repay a favor."

Hartley scratched his head. "I couldn't pay you much."

Alvin chuckled. "That's good, because I wouldn't take it anyway. Farmers need to take care of each other."

Hartley studied Alvin for a moment. "I appreciate that. It won't be until August. I have to get the lumber, and the shingles need time to dry."

"August works just fine. Just let me know when. How much wood do you need?"

Hartley looked at the hole in the roof of the barn. "I don't know exactly. I'll make a detailed list and drop it off."

Alvin reached out and shook Cy's hand. "You know where to find me."

There was only one other wagon at Hemmings when Alvin arrived. It was a beat-up buckboard with a hole in the side where the rot had been cut from one board. The wagon was pulled by a pair of gaunt looking chestnuts and Alvin felt sorry for the team. Clearly, they hadn't been fed well, and they looked sullen standing in the heat.

Alvin dismounted and was about to tie off his team when he heard his name.

"Where's your buddy McGinn?"

Alvin turned and saw Wendell Walked and his brother Emmitt. "I suspect he's working."

"I heard you married McCall's daughter. You must like that sweet young ass," said Wendell with a laugh.

"If you're looking for a fight. I'm too busy for the likes of you two. Perhaps another time." Alvin has been in enough scraps not to take the bait. There would be another time to settle scores, when the odds might be even.

"I think now's as good a time as any. Don't you Emmitt?"

Emmitt nodded and grinned. "Works for me. My afternoon is free."

Wendell made a show of rolling up his sleeves and a moment later, Emmitt followed his brother's lead.

They started forward, and Alvin assumed a fighting stance with his body compact and his fists raised close to his face. His chief concern was not letting one get behind him. If he struck fast, he might knock one down before the other one could strike.

The Walkers were cautiously closing the distance and Alvin made up his mind that Wendell was the leader and the bigger threat. He'd have to be first. "Let's have a go then, lass."

Wendell's face flushed, and he started forward.

Alvin prepared to strike, and the trio were startled by the sound of a loud bang on the side of the Walker's wagon.

"What the hell is going on here!?" Happy Hemmings stood at the back of the Walker's wagon wearing a leather apron and holding with a blacksmith's hammer in his right hand. "Wendell, is your business done?"

The rage drained from Wendell's face at the sight of Hemmings. "It is."

"Then it's time to be getting on with your business elsewhere. Don't you think?"

All the fight seemed to leave Wendell's body, like air from a balloon. "Yes, sir."

Happy moved closer to the Walker brothers. "I saw the whole thing. Next time you make trouble at my place, will be the last time you do business here."

"Yes, sir." Wendell said is something just above a whisper.

"Tell your father to get his account up to date, too. This is the last time you're getting credit here. Cash only if he's not caught up."

Wendell nodded and jumped onto the bench, while Emmitt untied the horses and climbed up beside him.

Hemmings glared at the two brothers. "And feed these god damned horses or that's the last team you'll buy from me."

Wendell's face started to flush again, but he turned and snapped the reins setting the wagon in motion.

"Thank you," Alvin said. "I told them I was too busy to fight, but they still feel hard done by from our last encounter."

"To hell with those two horse's asses. What are you here for?"

"Grain and Oats. Some meal for pigs and a salt lick if you have one."

Hemmings thought for a moment. "I have two broken licks. I could sell them to you for the price of one if that works?"

Alvin shrugged, "That would be grand."

"Put one in your pasture and one by your apple trees."

"The fence doesn't extend to the apple trees."

Hemmings laughed. "That one is for the deer. Put a little meat on your table this fall."

Alvin scratched his head. "Is that legal?"

"God no. But if they put every man in jail that poached a deer in these parts there'd be nothing but women, children and men too old to hunt," he laughed with a tremendous bellow. "Poached venison always tastes sweeter to me."

Alvin grinned. "I guess I'll find out."

Hemmings grew serious. "One more thing. When you go inside, tell them I said to give you an ax handle,"

"I have some at home I made from ash."

"I want you to keep one in the wagon with you. I wouldn't put it past those two to lay in wait for you somewhere."

Alvin sighed. "A solid stick of ash would be a prudent course to be sure."

Eleven

Mary marveled at the feeling of being pregnant. It made her chores much clumsier, but every time the baby moved, she rubbed her growing belly and smiled. Alvin did most of the milking even though she insisted that she was still capable, but she appreciated not having to get up and down from the milking stool.

She fed and watered the animals, tended the garden and of course cooked, but Alvin rushed about to make sure that she was never really straining herself around the farm. His helping bordered on smothering, but she knew his heart was in the right place, and he couldn't bear another loss like Edna and Nora. She felt like the loss of Parker Moreland's wife had made him paranoid that it might somehow happen to him.

On the previous weekend, he had taken her fishing on the stream that crossed the property and practically guided her every step of the way. "Look out for that limb," he'd say, or "Be careful, that rock looks slippery." At first, she found it a little amusing, but then it was just annoying. "For God's sake Alvin. Should we bring the pillows from the bed and a length of rope so you can wrap me up like a precious egg?"

"You are precious," he said. "A precious jewel."

She wasn't sure about all that, but she appreciated his admiration. When her father needed help at the Mountain to make a batch of Poteen, Alvin insisted that Catherine or one of the boys come stay with her so that she wouldn't be there alone. The minute they were done with the batch, he raced back to the farm to make sure everything was alright and resumed his smothering.

Since the beginning of May, she had only been to town twice. Her world was condensed to the property between their farm and her parents. She didn't mind it too much, but she was looking forward to the July 4th celebrations in Monroe. Mary had always loved the fireworks and the parade in town. The whole place came alive, and everyone tended to be in high spirits.

This year was going to be even more exciting, because Phillip was going to be boxing a young man from Watertown who was undefeated. Mary heard her brothers saying that most people thought this would be a fight that Phillip might not win. That seemed impossible to her. She knew that he had lost early in his career when he was still a teenager, but he boxed nearly every month and hadn't lost in over four years.

She admired Phillip, and her family adored him. Her brothers spoke as if every word from his mouth was pure gold and if

Phillip said the sun would rise in the west tomorrow, then that's where they'd be looking.

The sun baked down upon them and even with the top up, the ride to town was sweltering. Mary leaned back to keep her body in the little shade that the top provided, but she could feel the sweat running down her chest and under her growing breasts. At first, she was eager to have the growth, but now they seemed to be in the way and made her back ache when she was on her feet for long periods.

"Alvin. Can we stop at the lake on the way. I'm roasting. I just want to wade in a bit."

Alvin pulled a pocket watch from his pocket and studied the face. "I think we can spare a few minutes. We can water the horses on the way."

Mary took his hand and squeezed it. "Thank you. You spoil me, and I love it."

Alvin smiled and squeezed her hand back. "I pity Phillip. It's going to be hot fighting today."

Mary chuckled. "I don't think the heat bothers him. Nothing bothers him. Daddy says he's made of iron."

"Well, with enough heat, even iron melts."

The beach was already crowded, and those that weren't heading to town took advantage of the opportunity to get cool. Kids splashed in the water and mothers sat on the beach trying to shade themselves with big hats and umbrellas. It rarely reached the nineties in Maine, but the sun blazed away like nothing Mary could remember.

"Did it ever get this hot in Ireland?"

Alvin laughed. "No. It might reach eighty once every couple of years, but that would have been sandwiched between a week of rain on both ends. The weather there was very predictable. Rain and fog, followed by fog and rain. With the occasional few hours of sun thrown in. But we never had the snow and cold like here or in Canada."

Mary frowned. "I'd be miserable with that much rain."

"Lots of people there are, but they get used to it... and they drink a lot. So that helps."

They parked the wagon near a water trough, and Alvin pulled a tin bucket from the bed. He watered Pal and Chum stomped the ground impatiently. "Wait your turn, you sneaky bastard." Chum looked at Alvin with something akin to a glare and laid his ears back as if he might snap out at Alvin to bite him. "Have you ever seen an animal like this?" he asked Mary. "He'd love nothing better than to take a chunk of my arm out."

Mary moved beside Chum and stroked his neck. The gray pony relaxed, and his ears returned to their normal state. As she scratched at the areas behind the bridle, Chum drove his neck harder into her hands. Chum tilted his head and looked at Alvin in a way that seemed to be taunting him.

"He thinks he's stealing my wife. Look at him."

Mary laughed. "He could never steal me from you. He just likes me better, that's all."

"I'm going to be working on Cyr's timber this week, and he's going to be working every day. I can promise you that. I'll let Pal take it easy and work him and his chestnut friend until they learn to listen."

Mary frowned. "You're being spiteful. Don't be hard on them. They're good boys." She kissed Chum on the muzzle and scratched his nose.

Alvin shook his head. "I'll water him and join you on the beach if you want to cool off a bit."

"That sounds lovely. Come join me soon."

"I will. Just as soon as I get Loverboy a drink," he said, and Chum snorted and stomped his hoof. Mary walked toward the beach and Alvin whispered to Chum. "When you get old, I'll not send you to the glue factory. I'm going to make you into a stew, and we'll see who bites who then. Sneaky bastard."

Mary lifted her skirt to the middle of her thighs and waded into the Westview Lake. The water felt so good against her hot skin. As she stood holding her skirt, she could feel the heat penetrating her thick auburn hair and making her face hot. *The skirt will dry*, she thought to herself, and let it go. It floated on the water and slowly submerged. Mary took a deep breath and bent at the waist to dunk her head in the cool water. She felt the baby roll as the motion had put added pressure on her round belly. When she emerged, she stood up quickly and flipped the thick wet braid onto her back. It struck with a loud wet splat.

Mary smiled as the cold water ran down between her shoulders and she instantly felt the cool relief.

Alvin had removed his shoes and socks, then rolled his pant legs up to avoid walking around with wet feet all day. He waded to Mary who was watching a young mother with a naked infant dunking the baby up to her chest. The infant laughed with each dunk.

"What are you looking at?"

Mary turned and smiled. "Our future. That will be me next year."

Alvin watched the mother and child, then kissed her on the cheek. "Except it will be a boy."

"Huh. How do you know?"

He looked into her deep brown eyes and grinned. "I don't know. I just feel it."

Mary studied his face and knew somehow, he believed it and she couldn't help thinking that he was right. "Let's get to town, so we have time to sit in the shade before Phillip fights."

Alvin nodded. "Good idea." He held her hand as he escorted her from the water, and they collected their shoes. When they approached the wagon, Chum stood up straighter. "Loverboy is waiting for you."

Mary laughed. "He just knows a good thing when he sees it."

"Me too. That's why I'll never leave you. I'll never be this lucky again if I lived a hundred lifetimes."

Twelve

Alvin spread a blanket on the edge of the edge of the shade and held Mary's hand as she lowered herself to the ground.

"This is the perfect spot," he said.

Mary shrugged. "The shade is wonderful, but it does seem a little far away."

"Well, it's close enough to see and not get stepped on. Plus, I wouldn't want you to get sprayed with blood. At Phillip's last fight, I saw a glob of blood land on a woman's face."

Mary laughed. "Good God Alvin. I have helped to butcher animals, blood washes off."

"Maybe so. But I think it's going to get hotter as the afternoon wears on. It feels like we're losing the wee bit of breeze we have."

Mary smiled and patted the spot beside her on the blanket. "It's a fine view from here." Alvin sat, and she squeezed his hand. She wanted to kiss him on the cheek, but some frowned on public kissing, and she didn't want to do anything to embarrass him.

They sat watching the commotion as men hurried about, bringing a table and chairs to the judge's table and corner stools for the ring. Alvin recognized several of the locals among the crowd. The Major and Parker sat in the front row beside a thin man with dark hair and a pencil mustache, who Arthur had said was their lawyer, John Maxwell. Two of the Walkers and the big farm boy from the dance sat on the edge of a shed roof and occasionally shot Alvin a glare. Alvin smiled and tipped his cap once and once they realized he wasn't intimidated, they moved on to other interests.

When the clock struck the top of the hour, a man stepped onto the ring and dragged a microphone and cable to the center. He wore a straw hat, and a short-sleeved shirt. His suspenders curved around his potbelly, and he locked his free thumb under one side as he cleared his throat. "Ladies and gentlemen, welcome to the 8th annual July 4th Monroe Boxing Championship. This year features a match-up of light heavyweights." He unhooked his thumb and wiped sweat from his brow. "First the challenger. Hailing from Watertown," the crowd erupted in boos with a smattering of light applause. "Weighing in at one hundred and seventy-four pounds, with a record of eleven wins all by knockouts and no losses, Levi *Lightning* Levinsky!"

Levinsky emerged from the shed where the Walkers were sitting, wearing a blue silk robe with a Star of David on the right chest and the word Lightning across the back. Boos rained down and people yelled cruses and slurs. He stepped through the ropes and dropped the robe. He looked rugged, with long arms and broad shoulders. His face was a mask, and the crowd didn't appear to have any effect on his focus.

"Weighing in at one hundred and sixty-two pounds, with a record of forty-nine wins, one draw and one loss. Philip *the Hammer* Armstrong!"

When Phillip emerged, he wore no robe and trotted to the opposite corner to wild cheers from the crowd. When they locked eyes from their opposing corners Levinsky spat on the canvas ring.

Mary gasped. "My God. He's so much bigger than Phillip."

Alvin nodded. "He's giving up height, weight and age."

As the ring announcer introduced the referee and started laying out the rules. Alvin and Mary were joined by Daniel and Winslow. "Got room for two more?" asked Daniel, and plopped down beside them. Kevin was with Phillip's coach, working his corner ready with a bucket and sponge.

"Of course," replied Alvin and moved a little closer to Mary. "What are the odds?"

Winslow shrugged. "It depends on who you ask. Most are giving even money, but I heard a fella from Watertown giving two-to-one on the Jewish kid and the reverse odds from some locals."

"Makes sense I guess," said Alvin. "Phillip keeps winning, but the fights are getting closer and closer."

Daniel pulled a flask from his pocket and took a swig, then offered it to Alvin, who waved it off. "True enough. I thought that Lebanese guy had Phillip for sure, but he seems to last longer than the young guys.

The bell rang to start the round, and both men moved forward like big cats. Levinsky snapped off jab after jab, trying to use his reach advantage from the start. Phillip followed a missed jab with a hard shot to the body that made Levinsky recoil and keep a more measured attack.

When the bell rang to end the round, Phillip nodded as if to say good round and Levinsky growled then stomped to his corner.

Sweat was already pouring from Phillip's head as the July sun beat down upon his brow. Kevin offered him a water bottle, and he took two long gulps. When he looked across the ring, Levinsky sat glaring across the ring and knocked away the water when offered to him. The bell rang for round two, and Levinsky jumped to his feet and raced toward Phillip.

Phillip tried to side-step the cross, but Levinsky was lightning quick and caught Phillip's nose to a sickening squish a moment before the blood began to flow. Phillip staggered for a second and instinctively drove a hook into the lower ribs of Levinsky's left side. Levinsky bent unnaturally to the left and dropped his elbow to provide a little more protection. Alvin thought that Phillip may have broken Levinsky's ribs, but the big kid let loose with a barrage of punches sending Phillip into defensive moves to limit the pain. They exchanged blows and Phillip's actually looked relieved as the bell rung to end the round.

Phillip plopped down on the stool, and Kevin went to work on his nose. "Phil, you okay?"

Phillip nodded and wiped the blood from his nose. "I'll live," he nodded toward Levinsky, "That's one tough Jew right there." He took a drink again and saw Levinsky glaring and refusing to drink again. *That's right young buck*, he thought. *Let your pride block your common sense.*

Phillip had spent his whole life in the woods and understood the need for water, whether it was January or July.

Round after round proceeded in a similar matter, where Levinsky occasionally dealt a big blow and Phillip smashed away at Levinsky's body.

Towards the tenth round, the routine was broken. Phillip became the aggressor and charged Levinsky. He landed a stout right hook to Levinsky's side that caused a wince of pain, but as he connected, Levinsky caught Phillip with a cross to the jaw.

Phillip's legs began to buckle and Levinsky charged forward, throwing one wild punch after another. He caught Phillip in the face with a glancing blow that sent him reeling into the ropes. Levinsky stomped forward again to deliver the knockout.

Ding! Ding! Ding! At the sound of the end of the round, the referee jumped between the combatants and send Levinsky back to his corner.

Phillip dropped onto his stool with a thud and Kevin squeezed sponge after sponge of water over Phillip's head.

"Holy shit," said Winslow. "That kid is going to cost me a week's pay."

"It's not over yet," remarked Alvin. "Phillip will be looking for that cross the next time."

Winslow pulled a flask from his pocket and took a drink. "I hope you're right. This kid is one tough. S.O.B."

The bell rang to start the next round, and both men were back to the mundane routine of trading blows, with neither having much effect. Levinsky kept swinging for the knockout and Phillip continued to batter the younger fighter's left side. Alvin was sitting thirty feet away and already the bruising was visible on Levinsky's pounded ribs.

The fight continued this way until the seventeenth round. Levinsky was slow to rise from his stool and winced as he came to his feet. Phillip moved forward to meet him in the middle of the ring and Levinsky stomped forward in the same mechanical march he had had throughout the fight. But now it was much slower.

When Levinsky came into range, Phillip snapped off a jab that caught the younger fighter in the mouth and followed with a hook to the body that caused Levinsky to cry out in pain. He threw a wild left that missed Phillip by a foot. Phillip stepped in and landed shot after shot, but still, he couldn't break Levinsky. When the bell rang to end the round, Levinsky slowly walked to his corner and sat on the stool as his cornermen went to work on his bloody face. They poured water into his mouth, and it ran out onto his chest and down to his trunks.

"Jesus Christ," said Kevin. "Why don't they throw in the towel?"

Phillip took a drink of water and spit the rest into a bucket. "Nobody wants to lose their first fight. He wants me to knock him out to win."

Ding! Ding! Ding! Phillip got to his feet and inhaled deeply. Levinsky still sat on the stool glaring at him, but didn't rise.

"Hey fella. Let's go or I'll count you out," shouted the referee.

Levinsky raised his arms to pull himself up by the ropes and his eyes that were locked on Phillip rolled white inside of his head.

Phillip froze at the sight and a moment later Levinsky tumbled forward onto his face and didn't move.

The referee waved his arms and ended the fight to a wild cheer from the crowd. He strode forward and raised Phillip's arm high in the air. Phillip watched as Levinsky's corner jumped in and frantically began trying to revive him.

It was like being in a dream. Phillip watched and heard nothing. No cheers, no commotion, just a sound like the ocean in his head. He was startled to the present when Kevin dumped the bucket of water over his head.

When he shook the water from his head, he could hear that the cheers had subsided and now there were murmurs of concern and action as two burley orderlies from the hospital dragged Levinsky from the ring on a stretcher and raced to the back of a waiting ambulance.

Phillip said a silent prayer and made the sign of the cross.

"You don't go to church," said Kevin.

Phillip watched the ambulance race from the ring as people made way. "You don't need to be in a church for God to hear you."

Thirteen

It broke Mary's heart to see Phillip so hurt. He was the toughest man she had ever known in her young life, and now the air of invincibility seemed to be diminished. He won the fight, but he wasn't happy and the punishment on his body was profound. The entire left side of his face looked like an overstuffed sausage casing, and his eye was swollen completely shut.

When the fight ended, they had rushed Levinsky to the hospital. Phillip did his best to accommodate the friends who cheered him on, but after about five minutes in the crowd with the sun beating down on his head, he staggered a little and fell onto his backside with an ignominious thud. Only the bottom rope kept him from falling another three feet onto the ground.

People rushed to help him, and the Monroe police chief drove him to the hospital in a police car to avoid waiting for another ambulance. Kevin and Winslow rode with him, and waited for the word to be able to visit.

Dr. Corbett and Dr. McDermott ran the hospital jointly, but they were tied up trying to stabilize Levinsky, so they sent their new man, Dr. Turner to treat Phillip. He didn't want any distractions, so he made Kevin and Winslow wait outside.

When Dr. Turner returned Phillip was with him. He had a small bandage on his left eye where they had drained the blood enough for him to see.

"You wanna' get outta' here?" asked Winslow.

Phillip shook his head. "I want to wait until I know he's alright."

A man and woman in their forties sat at the far end of the waiting room, with a couple of teenaged boys standing beside them. Philip figured they must be Levinsky's parents and walked over.

The man met Phillip's eyes and rose. "You're a fine fighter. The best my Levi has ever fought."

Phillip nodded. "He's young, but he's one of the toughest men I ever fought."

The man chuckled a little. "He's always been a fighter. We live in a mixed neighborhood, Jews and Lebanese. We may be from the same part of the world, but old animosities die hard."

"What's your name?" asked Phillip.

"Jacob Levinsky." He turned to his family. "This is my wife Sallee and my younger sons, Samuel and Ezra."

Phillip met the gaze of each one. "I'm pleased to meet you. Have the doctors given you any word at all?"

Jacob sighed. "No. Just that he has a lot of internal bleeding. You worked his left side pretty good."

"The sun didn't help. But to be honest, it was my only choice. If I stayed outside his range, he would have caved my face in." Phillip turned to the right. "Nearly did."

The discussion was broken by the appearance of Dr. McDermott. He was a large man with white hair and blue eyes. His complexion was red and made both his eyes and hair look brighter from the contrast. "Mr. Levinsky?"

Jacob stepped forward and nodded holding his breath.

McDermott nodded a little. "He's going to be alright.

The Levinskys let out a collective sigh of relief.

McDermott held up a finger to squelch the celebration. "He had several broken ribs and a lacerated his spleen."

"What does that mean?" asked Sallee.

"He's going to be more susceptible to infections. He may have pain in his abdomen for the rest of his life. Even more so after physical activity. His recovery is going to be the better part of a year, I'm afraid."

"But he's a stonemason," replied Jacob.

McDermott shook his head. "He's not anymore. Or at least he won't be for a very long time. The important thing is that he's alive and will likely have a long life."

"Of course you're right. Thank you, doctor."

McDermott shook Jacob's hand and turned to leave.

"Doctor. Can we see him?"

McDermott nodded. "Give us a bit. He's just out of surgery, but we'll send a nurse when he's ready."

"Thank you."

McDermott disappeared through the door and Phillip reached into his pocket and produced a large gold medal on a long ribbon. He looked at Jacob and extended his hand. "I want Levi to have this."

Jacob studied the medal. It was inscribed with CHAMPION and the day's date.

"I don't understand. You won the fight."

Phillip shook his head. "I was saved by that bell. He could have blown on me and knocked me out. I was out on my feet. Ten seconds more and he would have had his twelfth win. An even dozen knockouts."

Jacob shook his head. "I know him. He won't take it."

"I won't take it back. He won it. He was the better fighter. I was just the more experienced."

Jabob ran his fingers over the medal and slipped it into his pocket. "Thank you. I'll be sure he takes it."

Phillip forced a smile. "Good. I have to be leaving, but please know he'll be in my thoughts and prayers tonight."

"We'll keep you in ours as well. If you ever come to Watertown, please look us up. We live in an apartment right above the Woolworth's on Maine Street. It's apartment one."

Phillip reached out and shook Jacob's hand. "I will certainly do that." He turned and pointed to Winslow and Kevin. "Let's head home."

Winslow picked up his hat and yanked it onto his head. "Wanna grab a drink somewhere?"

Phillip shook his head. "Nah. I need water, not spirits."

"Fair enough. I'll fill a jug with water before we go," replied Winslow.

"Sounds good."

Phillip sat on the bench of the wagon without making a sound. That wasn't typical of him. Most fight nights ended with a few rounds of drinks and a steak dinner if his jaw was well enough to still chew.

As they passed the Lakeview Country Club a few people congratulated him on the win and others just stared and whispered. He wasn't sure what they'd have to whisper about, but honestly, he didn't care. Phillip was well respected and answered to no one. He watched as they approached the beach and saw two children splashing in the water with a baby girl sitting on the beach at the water's edge.

Phillip became animated and tapped Winslow on the arm. "Hey. Stop here."

"Why?"

"I want to. So just stop."

Winslow pulled back on the reins and called out. "Whoa. Easy boys."

The wagon came to a stop and Phillip jumped off landing hard. He let out an audible wince when the shock of the impact came rushing through his battered frame. He walked toward the water and removed his shirt, shoes and socks, then placed them under his arm, heading to the beach. It was evening and the sun hung just above the western horizon. The clouds had orange and purple highlights. He tried to think about how many thousands of sunsets he had seen in his life, but almost immediately he realized that it was one of the most beautiful he had ever seen.

Phillip laid his shirt and shoes away from the waterline and waded into his waist. When the cool water hit his bare skin, he reached in and flung water on himself, then dropped beneath the surface. Everything was muffled and he tried to look around. He could see rocks all around, but not much of everything else.

Phillip could feel the tension in his muscles and clenched his fist, then tilted his face toward the surface and screamed with all of his might. The noise sounded unnatural in the water, and he watched the blast of bubble flying toward the surface.

When he popped up, Winslow and Kevin were at the beach watching to be sure he didn't drown. Phillip stayed in the water up to his chin letting the cold from the water penetrate his tired body. He felt at peace.

He dunked himself one more time and shot to the surface. The water ran down his back as if it was washing him clean of all his burdens.

When he trudged to the shore Kevin handed him his shirt. "How's the water?"

"Refreshing." Phillip slipped his short on and collected his shoes, then walked to the wagon. Winslow and Kevin followed in silence.

When they started down the road again Phillip spoke up. "I'm done."

"Done what?" asked Winslow.

"Fighting. At least professionally. It doesn't appeal to me anymore."

Kevin looked at Phillip in disbelief. "Are you sure? You're still a young man."

Phillip nodded and smiled. "I am. Don't know why, but I'm at peace and I want to stay that way."

Winslow shrugged. "You went out on top. Good a time as any I suppose."

"Feels right."

They rode along in silence for a ways and Winslow slapped his leg. "Dammit."

"What wrong?" asked Kevin.

"I wish I would have bet more."

Phillip chuckled. "Then you would have been shitting your pants when that kid almost knocked me out."

Kevin studied Phillip for a moment. "Was it really that close?"

Phillip nodded. "I was out on my feet. My mind wanted to punch, but my legs were as soft as jelly and my arms wouldn't move. If that bell hadn't rung, I'd have been done."

"He didn't help himself refusing water," added Winslow.

"Young and foolish, I guess. Sometimes we have to learn things the hard way to learn anything at all."

Kevin laughed. "Ha. Hell, I still haven't learned anything."

Phillip shrugged. "Give it time."

Fourteen

S weat dripped off the end of Alvin's nose as the August sun beat down on him like a hammer. He tried to remember a day as hot in Ireland, but none came to mind. Cy and Alvin had stripped away the rotted shingles, only to find rotted boards. When they removed the rotted wood, they found roof timbers in a state so punky that a single blow from a hammer could knock away a chunk of wood the size of his fist.

They consulted with Arthur and a couple of other locals who had experience raising barns and all agree that sister timbers was the only logical solution. They cut long straight beams to run beside the soggy ones and joined them through the wood with thick wooden pegs and long iron bolts.

Alvin stood on the scaffolding that Cy had rigged to the side of the barn and handed lumber up the roof to Cy. He peeked over the edge, and it seemed quite high. From the ground to the eaves was at least fourteen feet, and the eaves to the top of the first rafter was another twelve.

With every step, he could feel a bounce in the large planks that served as the decking from which he worked, and he started to question whether or not the thickness was enough to hold his weight. They had rigged safety ropes around their waists in case some one fell, but even that felt a little suspect as to whether or not it could hold a man in a free fall. He spat off the side and a second or so later he thought he could hear a faint splat.

Alvin handed Cy the last board and climbed onto the roof with him to set the boards. They had Sampsons saw out the lumber with a shiplap edge so that each board overlapped the next. That way when the boards inevitably shrunk from drying, they wouldn't be left with a gap for rain to sneak through and start the whole process over again.

Alvin liked working with Cy. He was funny and patient, and he respected Alvin's input into the best ways to tackle a problem. Each man tapped his board into place and when the gap was sealed, Cy would call out. "Like it?"

"I do," Alvin would reply.

"Then nail it." Both men would start driving nails in neat rows, moving to the next timber when their row was complete until they had the board fully secured. They set the next board and Alvin leaned in to inspect the joint.

"Like it?"

"I do," said Alvin and he began to hammer.

He heard a voice call from below. "Have you hit your thumb with a hammer yet?!" It was Mary with Toto prancing along beside her.

Alvin shook his head and laughed. "No not yet!" He grabbed a nail and started driving it. On his third swing sweat dripped into his eye and the hammer glanced off the nail, landing squarely on the end of the thumb that was holding it straight. He winced in pain and brought the smashed thumb to his mouth.

Mary stood on the ground laughing and shaking her head. "I'll be sure not to ask you if you fell off the roof yet!"

Alvin shook his hand trying to bring some feeling other than pain back to his throbbing thumb. "Thanks! I'd appreciate that!"

Mary held a basket high in the air. "I have some food and drinks for you."

Alvin turned to Cy. "Want to finish this board and eat?"

Cy shrugged. "The board is fine. Let's eat. I'm starving and my mouth is so dry my tongue feels like firewood."

Both men climbed down their ladders to the deck of the scaffold and Alvin untied his tether and started down the ladder. As he climbed, he heard the groan of the planks as Cy made his way across. Dirt and sawdust fell between the planks with each step.

Alvin saw him mount the ladder above him and started down a little quicker.

When they reached the ground, Alvin pointed to the deck. "We should add some more planking. That had an uncomfortable degree of bounce to it."

Cy studied the structure. "It's a sturdy frame. Besides, that's all the planks I had left. It does take a bit to get your sea legs on that deck though. It'll be fine. Plus, we'll be shingling soon, and then we'll be done. It's held us this far."

Alvin looked the structure over again. "We should rig a derrick though to haul those shingles. Otherwise, we'll be dragging them up the ladders, tied to our backs."

Mary flipped a cloth from the top of the basket. "Are you going to eat or debate?"

Alvin saw bottle necks poking over the edge and grabbed two, handing one to Cy. "Cold tea with honey. Nothing better on a hot day. I like it with milk too, but it might curdle in this heat."

Cy pulled the stopper and took a long drink. He swirled the liquid in the bottom to dissolve some of the settled honey. "That is nice. Thank you."

Mary smiled at the complement and moved the basket closer so that they could see the contents. "I have chicken sandwiches with pickles and tomatoes."

They each took a sandwich and began chomping away. Cy followed a bite with a swallow of tea. "I'm so hungry I could eat boiled horse hide."

Alvin took slow bites and tried to chew deliberately. There was something about working in the heat that made it difficult for him to eat. He finished the first half of the sandwich easily enough but started choking down the second half.

Mary studied the pair as they ate. "You both look pretty red. Be sure to drink your fill before you go back up there."

"Don't worry darlin', I'm about to cool down. Just watch." Alvin walked to the well head and began pumping the long grey handle. Water poured from the spout, and he slipped a two-gallon pail under the flow and pumped away. When the bucket was nearly full, he stopped, and the flow moved first to a trickle, and then some drops. Alvin picked up the bucket and slurped water until he couldn't drink anymore. He smiled at Mary and upended the entire pail over his head soaking his hair, shirt and pants. "Woo! That's brisk...now give us a kiss love."

Mary took a step back and held her arms extended. "I don't think so. I'll kiss you when you get home. I don't want to get all wet."

"Are you sure? It's quite refreshing."

"Positive. I'm going to head back. Bring the basket home with you and I'll send you with something for lunch tomorrow."

Cy smiled and took another half of a sandwich. "Thank you so much Mary. My wife is in town, so I've been fending for myself."

Mary smiled. "You're welcome. Please see that he doesn't fall off the roof. He said it's happened before."

Alvin looked up at the scaffolding. "Don't worry love. We're tied off and this is about three times the height I fell from, so I'm being extra careful."

"Well, you can do a whole lot of amazing things, but I doubt flying is one of them." She kissed his cheek and gave two quick whistles. Toto raced around the corner of the barn, ready to make the trip home.

Alvin watched smiling, as she waddled to the road and walked at a leisurely pace while Toto raced ahead and explored the ditch.

Cy watched the tree line like something was out of place. "Let's get the rest of these boards on and rig your derrick. Probably get a shower this afternoon or evening, so we'll save the shingling for tomorrow."

Alvin searched the sky. There was nothing but white clouds and hot sun. "I don't see any threat of rain."

Cy pointed to the woods. "See those maples?"

"Of course I do."

"See how they're showing us the backs of their leaves?"

"I think that's just the breeze. A tree can't move on its own."

Cy chuckled. "It's a figure of speech. But you are right, the breeze is blowing and when it blows like that, it means rain is coming." He took a big bite of sandwich and sipped some tea.

Alvin shook his head. "That's an old wives' tale."

Cy swallowed and took a big gulp. "I'll bet you a quart of your poteen against a pint of bourbon that it rains tonight."

"A quart versus a pint? That doesn't sound fair."

"Well bourbon has to be aged in a barrel. You just stir yours in a cauldron up on a hill. So, bourbon is more expensive now isn't it."

Alvin thought about that for a minute. "I suppose so...you're on."

When Alvin got home, he tended the animals. Mary had already done most of the chores, but she found it harder and harder to do the milking, so Alvin insisted on being the one to do it.

He was rhythmic in his milking and became so lost in his thoughts that he nearly tumbled over backwards when the thunderclap rang out over head. *Still no rain though*, he thought and continued to milk. When he stopped, he heard a splat, then another and another until the sound was like steak sizzling in a hot pan. It was raining.

Alvin nodded with satisfaction and covered the milk pail with a cloth. "Huh. Sounds like home." He rushed from the barn to the porch to get the milk out of the rain and unbuttoned his shirt, pulling it off and tossing it on the porch as well.

The rain felt good. He was out a quart of liquor, but he didn't care. The rain made it feel like all his worries were washing away.

Alvin stepped into the downpour and let the sweet summer rain pelt as he moved his body to let every part be washed.

"What are you doing?" he heard Mary call out from the porch.

"Just enjoying the bath. Would you be carin' to join me?"

Mary frowned and rubbed her belly. "I don't believe I'd care for that at all. It's hard enough getting in and out of clothes in my state, I can't imagine it if they were wet."

Alvin smiled and shrugged. "I can help you out of your clothes."

"Huh! That's what brought me to this state in the first place."

Fifteen

Mary woke early as the first rays of sunlight pierced the gap in the bedroom curtains. She tried to hide her face in the blanket, but the light had already woken her. Now the baby pushed hard up under her ribs making her full bladder feel as though it might burst.

Not so hard little one. I don't want a mess before I can get downstairs, she thought. She peeked over to see if Alvin was still asleep, but he was already up and tending to the milking. She pulled his pillow close and inhaled. She loved that scent. It was him and it always made her feel better to have him near, even if it was by scent alone.

She dressed and made her way to the summer kitchen. Alvin had already started a fire in the stove and a kettle sat a little away from the heat with a light wisp of steam rising from the spout.

"Nearly hot enough for tea", she said aloud and slid it back over the fire. Alvin was a creature of routine if nothing else. Every morning, he had two eggs, some fried bread or biscuits and tea. At times when they had bacon or ham available, he would add a bit of meat, but he never went without the three. He called it his holy breakfast trinity.

Mary sliced some bread and set it aside then collected some eggs from the metal basket that sat on the shelf. She had always enjoyed tending chickens as a girl and had won several ribbons at the Monroe fair for her entries. She felt the baby kick and she smiled. "Someday perhaps you'll enter chickens too," she said and smiled.

Her thought was broken by the sound of footsteps coming in from the barn. Alvin carried a pail of fresh milk covered with cloth to keep dirt from falling in. "Lot's of cream for butter," he said and plopped the pail on the floor. Alvin moved close and wrapped his arms around Mary kissing her cheek. "You get more beautiful every day."

"Huh. I guess you like em plump to bursting."

"I love you however you are." He slid his hand onto her stomach and felt the baby kick.

Mary gasped a little. "She's telling you hands off. It's that type of thing that brought us to this condition in the first place."

Alvin frowned. "You felt that kick. That's a son to be sure."

"Go wash up and I'll bring you some breakfast in a few minutes."

Alvin kissed her again and brough the pail inside. He washed in the sink and sat down by the window with his Audubon book of birds and lit his pipe. When he left the barn, his attention had been drawn to a loud sharp call from the lilac tree. Perched on a branch was a black bird with orange and white stripes across its shoulders. At first, he was convinced that he had seen his first oriole, but the illustrations showed him it was a cousin of sorts, the red winged blackbird and he began reading everything he could about his new friend.

Mary felt a sense of amusement watching him smoke and read his book. Every new bird was like finding a lost treasure to him. Soon he'd regale her with facts about the habitat and mating rituals of the species.

She wrapped the pan handle in a thick cloth and brought the pan to the table. "Come eat," she said smiling. "It's how you like it."

The smell of freshly toasted bread made Alvin tap his pipe out and close his book. "I need a good breakfast. I want to help Hartley get his roof finished before it gets too hot. That rain soaked everything, so it'll be like working in a hot spring by noon."

"Well make sure you drink plenty of water. I don't want you falling off the roof."

Alvin chuckled. "I tie myself off. I don't mind the height, but why chance it."

Mary kissed his cheek and poured him a cup of tea. "Good. Safe is always good."

Alvin gobbled down his breakfast, mopping every bit of yolk with his bread. "I'm going to saddle Buddy. I'll be back in for kiss before I go."

"Okay love. I'm afraid it's just tomato sandwiches and a half a jar of pickles today for lunch."

"It'll be too hot to eat anyway. That will be refreshing," he said and kissed her cheek.

Mary cleared the dishes and pumped a little water into the sink for washing. While she wiped the pan, she laughed aloud listening to Alvin curse as he tried to saddle the pony.

"That's not a good start," she said aloud.

When she moved the pan to the drying rack, she felt a trickle of water running down the inside of her leg. "My God, I've wet myself." She waddled toward the commode that held the chamber pot, but before she could get there, she felt the gush and heard the water splat onto the kitchen floor.

"Alvin!" Mary grabbed a kitchen towel from the counter and started wiping her inner legs. She wasn't sure if he had heard her, so she moved to the door and yelled again. "Alvin! I need you!"

He turned and saw Mary in the doorway holding her round belly with eyes as big as saucers.

"Mary!" he sprinted toward the porch and made the leap without touching a single step. "Are you okay/! Is it the baby?!"

Mary smiled. "You need to go get my Ma. It's time."

Alvin stared dumbly as he tried to comprehend what she was saying and what he should be doing. "What if the baby comes while I'm gone?"

"It won't. It doesn't work that fast. But she'll be here today. I feel certain of that."

Alvin nodded with understanding. "Okay. I'll go now. Lie down and rest. I'll be back as quick as a rabbit."

Mary grinned. "I know you will."

Alvin raced toward Buddy and the chestnut flinched at his approach. "You son of a bitch, you want to run every time I ride you. Run now." Alvin stepped into the stirrup and flung himself onto Buddy's back with the reins in his hand and bellowed "Ha!"

Buddy galloped out of the yard and tore down the dirt road like his tail was on fire with Alvin crouched down behind his neck.

Mary rubbed her stomach and smiled. "Thank goodness your father is a good rider. The pony might break his neck if he throws him."

Mary sat in the rocking chair watching out the window for his return. She and her mother had worked out the plan well in advance and Agnes Murphy, a neighbor further down the road would come assist with the delivery. Agnes had helped deliver a dozen or more babies around Howell Hill and Sparta.

Before she could see anyone on the road, she saw a cloud of dust rising above the tree line. "He's going to run that pony to death."

Alvin cleared the tree line and led Arthur, Cat and Daniel following in the buck board. A single horse carriage trailed them with a small woman at the reins.

"It's a parade for you little one," she said and chuckled. The laugh turned to a grimace when the contraction hit. Mary tried breathing through pursed lips and clutched the arm of the chair to weather the wave of pain. It passed and bit by bit her muscles returned to relaxation. "And just in time it would seem."

Alvin rode into the yard and jumped off Buddy, tying him to the trough. Buddy's coat glistened and foam crept from everywhere leather touched him. Alvin gave him a pat on the neck and nodded. "Good lad."

Mary shook her head as he rushed across the yard and stumbled trying to jump the porch steps. She fought back a laugh when he grabbed his shin and cursed under his breath.

Alvin burst through the door out of breath. "Is the baby here?!"

"No, it'll be some time, yet you know."

"Thank God. They're all just behind me."

"We have time Alvin. Everything will be fine. I promise."

Alvin took a deep breath and relaxed. "Okay. I'll send word to Cy that I won't be down. Arthur said Daniel can help him today."

"Good. Make yourself busy. I can't have you hovering all day, like some nervous Nellie. It makes me tense."

Alvin nodded. "Okay. I'll help settle the animals."

She watched as he met everyone in the yard and unhooked the horses. Arthur helped Cat from the wagon, and she felt a sense of relief to see her mother and Agnes coming up the porch steps.

Mary rubbed her belly again and smiled. "I'll see you soon little one."

Sixteen

Alvin paced up and down the porch with his hands clasped behind his back and his pipe clenched between his teeth. Every few minutes he heard Mary wail when the wave of the contractions hit.

He looked at the porch ceiling as if he could somehow see into the room above. "My God that sounds painful."

Arthur chuckled. "It'd stave the hell outta me."

Alvin frowned. His mind was far too occupied to make jokes.

"Ease up lad. Women have been having babies for thousands of years. My Mary will be no different."

"In my mind I know that. It's just my experience and Parker's wife... It makes me a wreck."

Arthur produced a brown bottle from beside his chair. "Have a sip. It'll calm your nerves."

Alvin took the bottle and sniffed. "Whiskey?"

"Canadian. I picked up some off from the LaCroix brothers. I was saving it for a special occasion. Don't get any more special than this."

"I suppose not." Alvin brough the bottle to his lips and took a long swallow. "Oh. That's nice."

Arthur patted the empty chair next to him. "Sit with me."

Alvin felt like a bottle that had been shaken about to blow its cork, but he forced himself to sit.

"Take another drink and have a smoke with me."

Alvin picked up the bottle and drank another taste, then repacked his pipe and lit up. "I feel a little better."

"Of course you do. If this lasts long into the day, you might busy yourself with tasks or tending to the animals."

"How long does it take? Do you think it will be all day?"

"No. Kevin was quick. I think about three or four hours. Dan took longer. His head was the size of a turnip and damned near split Cat in two. Mary was quick. I barely got the handywoman to the house and half an hour later, there she was."

Alvin sat back and puffed his pipe contemplating various times between contractions. Were they getting closer or were they still several minutes apart. "I hope she doesn't suffer long. It's hard to hear her crying out."

"She'll be fine son. Mary is a strong girl."

Alvin nodded and puffed his pipe. When he reached for the bottle again, he was startled by Mary's cry. It seemed louder than before, and he could hear Cat and Mrs. Murphy calling out instructions although he really couldn't hear what they were saying over Mary's cry. He jumped to his feet and looked at the porch ceiling again. "I think the baby is almost here."

"I think you're right. Better put the bottle away or we'll be chided for being drunk at the baby's birth." Arthur slid the bottle behind the chair and covered it with a wooden box he had been using as a footstool.

Alvin hopped off the porch down to the lawn and looked up at the window to their bedroom. Mary gave a long, loud scream as if she were lifting a train and a moment later it was quiet. No more screaming. No more barking encouragement. Just silence. Alvin felt a wave of anxiety and for a moment he saw the broken teacup in his mind's eye. Then his lungs filled to the point of bursting when he heard the unmistakable sound of a wailing child.

Arthur walked down the steps and put his arm around Alvin. "Thank you, son."

"For what?"

"You've given Catherine something to occupy herself with besides me. It'll greatly increase my leisure time." He slapped Alvin on the back and busted out in a booming laugh.

Catherine came to the window and yelled done. "Stop that horseplay and come meet your son and grandson."

Alvin looked at Arthur and smiled. "A son. Someone to carry on the McGinn name."

"Don't let him grow up to be a Nancy like your brothers-in-law."

Alvin laughed. "I won't. I promise."

When Alvin entered the room, Mary held the baby stroking his wet wispy hair. "He's beautiful," she whispered.

Alvin choked back tears. "Like his mother." He felt his chest tighten, holding back a wave of emotion. He was happy and relieved at the same time. The baby looked pink and plump and perfect.

Arthur patted Alvin on the back. "What are you going to name him?"

He smiled and looked at Mary. "Have you decided?"

"Alder."

"Alder? Like the tree?" asked Catherine.

Mary smiled and moved her pinky into the baby's tiny hand. "Yes. I wanted an A name, like Arthur, Ambrose and Alvin. I like Alders. They grow close together and I loved playing in them as a child. Alder Richard. For Alvin's friend. If he never met Richard, he may never have met me."

Alvin felt a tear run down his cheek. He couldn't imagine a better name. In that moment he wished Richard was here to see his namesake. "That's a grand name, for a grand boy."

Mary smiled and held out her hand. "You were right about it being a boy. Now come meet your son."

Alvin grinned from ear to ear. "There's a first time for everything." He leaned in and kissed her cheek, the slowly took the child from her arms. "This is the first time I've held a child since Emily was a baby."

Alder let out a small coo as Alvin pulled him close to his chest. "He's perfect, love. You did good."

Mary reached out and stroked his arm. "We did good."

Alvin moved toward Arthur so he could get a look at the baby.

"We'll give you a few years and then we'll start teaching you to hunt and fish and brew the poteen."

Cat frowned. "You'll do no such thing. I won't have my grandson poaching and breaking law as a child. He'll be the first McGinn or McCall man to go to college and make something of himself. You mark my words. They'll achieve something in life. More than we ever did. He'll go to college and be rich as a Moreland."

Arthur scowled and pretended to spit on the floor. "If he turns out like a Moreland, I'll kick his ass myself."

"Daddy! Don't talk like that. No one is kicking anyone. Especially my beautiful boy."

Arthur dropped his head and softened, "I'm sorry. It's your mother what set me off with all her Moreland talk."

Catherine huffed. "Huh. Don't blame me for your foul temperament."

Agnes Murphy had been watching the debate with some amusement and cleared her throat. "Ahem. Arthur, could I trouble you to give me a ride back to my place. I have animals to tend and children to feed."

Arthur collected himself. "Oh yes, of course Agnes. Thank you for all of your help. Let me go harness the buggy."

"Thank you, Arthur."

"Of course. I'll hold him later."

Artur left to harness his rig. Alvin raised the child to his slips and kissed him gently on the forehead. "I'm so happy to meet you son." He gave the baby to Catherine and moved to Mary's side. "Thank you love. He's the greatest gift I have ever received." Alvin leaned in and kissed her lips. They were dry from her efforts, and her face was wet with sweat, but when he kissed her, it was like the first time they kissed in the woods, and he felt his heart melt.

"You're welcome. Now we have a family."

The moment was broken by a commotion in the yard. Daniel had returned in a fury and Arthur barked at him for riding the horse so hard. "What ails you boy! For Christs' sake!"

Alvin moved to the window and saw Daniel out of breath talking with Arthur.

Arthur turned to the window. "Alvin! Get down here! There's been an accident!"

Alvin and Daniel drove the buckboard pulled by Buddy and Chum as fast as he dared to on Howell Hill Road. When they pulled into Hartley's place, his wife was kneeling beside him crying and his son Everett who was not quite two cried because his mother was crying.

Daniel had been hauling bundles of shingles up to Cy by the derrick and when he reached to pull the load to the scaffolding, he slipped on the wet planks and plummeted twenty feet to the ground.

When he hit, Daniel heard a loud snap followed by a sickening thud. At first, he thought Hartley had just had the wind knocked out of him, but he saw Cy's right leg pinned in an unnatural position under his body. He had broken his leg, and blood was oozing from his mouth. Daniel rushed to his aid, and he coughed in a spray of blood that looked to be much more than a bit tongue.

When Cy couldn't talk, Daniel ran to get his wife and rushed back to the farm for help.

Alvin jumped from the buckboard and rushed to his friend. "How bad is he hurt?!"

Julia sniffed and wiped her nose on her sleeve. "I don't know. He only cries out in pain. He hasn't said anything yet."

Alvin looked at the leg and it remined him of Romeo, but there was no bone sticking out. "Christ. Daniel, can you spread the blankets under the bench and let's get him to the back of the wagon. Bring one to help us lift him."

"I will." Daniel bolted for the wagon and jumped up into the bed and piled the blankets into a neat rectangle."

Alvin took Julia's hand. "Get the baby and jump up in the bed. We'll bring him to the hospital in town."

Julia nodded and tried to organize her thoughts. She picked up Everett and lifted him to the back of the wagon, then climbed up.

Alvin took the blanket and laid it beside Cy. "Come on. Let's get him on the blanket and we can lift him together."

Daniel nodded in understanding. When they moved Cy to the blanket he cried out in a whimper without opening his eyes. Together the lifted him and slid his torso onto the wagon then Daniel jumped up and pulled him in the rest of the way.

Alvin climbed onto the bench. "I'll take them to town. Can you tend to his animals and tell the farm I'll be back as soon as I can."

Daniel nodded. "Of course. Mrs. Hartley, I'll take care of everything here."

Julia wiped tears from her eyes. "I don't care about those damned animals. I just want my husband safe."

Alvin reached back and placed a hand on her shoulder. "I'll do my best. I promise." He snapped the reins and the team bolted forward at a fast trot. Alvin looked to the sky. "Edna. Please keep my friend safe." He crossed himself and blew a kiss to the heavens.

Seventeen

Mary lay in bed with Alder swaddled beside her and Cat asleep in the rocking chair. She heard the unmistakable creaking of the stairs as Alvin tried to enter as quietly as possible. The quiet creaking was followed by a loud thud when Alvin tripped on the top step.

She heard him cry out, "son of a whore" in a loud whisper and it made Mary sit up in bed. She was frustrated with him for leaving them a few minutes after the baby was born, but then she thought back to their trip to the Monroe fair, and how he had paid the Jones widow ten dollars purely out of principle. It was one of the things she loved about him the most.

Alvin lifted the latch and crept in quietly by lamp light. "You're awake," he whispered.

Mary nodded and pointed at Cat. Alvin gently shook his mother-in-law. "Catherine. Why don't you go the day bed downstairs you'll sleep better there."

Catherine opened one eye and nodded. "You're on duty from here." She rose and took his lamp then walked from the room dragging a quilt behind her.

"How's Alder."

"Sleeping. He just ate an hour ago."

Alvin slid into bed beside her and kissed her cheek. "I'm sorry to have left like that. Are you cross?"

Mary was cross, but she was proud of him too. "No. Not really. How is Cy?"

Alvin took a deep breath and exhaled. "He's alive and the doctor said he may make a full recovery someday, but he'll be in the hospital for months. He broke his leg and his back."

Mary gasped, "Can he walk?"

"He can move his foot on the leg that's not broke and he has feeling. The doctor said it's a miracle. He fell at least sixteen feet. Maybe twenty."

Mary crossed herself. "God was watching over him."

"I suspect so. But the doctor says he won't be able to work any time before spring," said Alvin.

Mary's eyes grew wide. "Oh, my goodness. We'll need to help them. How will they get their harvest in?"

Alvin kissed her cheek. "We won't let them fail. I already reached out to Elias to have him help. You tend to that baby, and I'll tend to these farms."

Mary looked at him and wondered if she could love anyone more. He had suffered great losses in his life already and still he looked to take care of others. She thought for a long moment.

Perhaps one needs to understand the depths of a loss like that to be truly generous. "I'll be fine. Besides, my mother will be here more to help. If Julia needs help with canning, we can go down and do it together."

Alvin chuckled. "Bastard."

"What's so funny?"

"Your father thanked me for giving Cat something to occupy herself besides him. Just never thought she'd be under my foot."

Mary gasped and made a fist, then hammered him in the arm. "I'm telling her you said that, and what Daddy said too. You'll both be in trouble."

Alder woke and cried.

"See what you've done. You've woken the baby."

Mary picked up Alder and slipped him onto her breast. He fumbled clumsily trying to latch on until Mary slid the nipple into his tiny mouth. "Be thankful you're not the one who has to feed him."

When Mary brought Alder downstairs the next morning, Catherine had already gotten up and started the stove in the summer kitchen. "I'm making a batch of biscuits. The men can take them down to the Hartley place."

"I'm sure they'll appreciate that. I'd like to go and see if I can help. But I'm too tired and too sore."

Catherine kneaded her biscuit dough almost mechanically. She had made so many biscuits in her life that she mixed the ingredients by sight and feel. "Agnes left a tea of sorts for you to take a few times a day. It'll help you heal."

Mary sat and gently rocked Alder in the rocking chair. "What's in it?"

"Raspberry leaf, chamomile and a tiny bit of comfrey. She also left a bottle of witch hazel to take in a bath."

Mary frowned. We usually just wash at the sink or in a basin. We don't have a tub yet."

"You can use your wash tub. I'll help you in and out."

Mary sighed. "Thanks Ma. I'm glad you're here."

"I'm happy to be here. I have a grandchild to cuddle, so I'm content."

"Well, I appreciate it. I have no idea what I'm supposed to be doing."

Catherine smiled. "Just feed him when he's hungry. Change him when he's soiled and get rest when he's sleeping. God knows you'll need it." Catherine rolled the dough and began cutting it into circles. "Oh, and have Alvin get you a tin of bag balm next time he goes to Hemmings."

"Why is the cow's udder cracked again?"

"No but yours might be. Just put a very thin layer on the nipple he's not feeding on. Works on us just as well as it does the cow."

Mary laughed. "I supposed it would." Mary laid Alder on the daybed and stretched her back. "Can I help with the biscuits?"

"No. But you can go check for eggs. I'll watch the baby. Just wash your hands good when you get back."

Mary felt a sudden rush of anxiety. This would be the first moment that he had not been with her since he was born. "Are you sure that's okay. What if he wakes up?"

Catherine wiped her hands on her apron and smiled. "I raised the three of you. We'll be fine. Besides, it's okay for a baby to cry a bit. If you hold them all the time, they get greedy and then they hang on you every minute when they are older. Danny was terrible. He wanted to feed every hour and sometimes you just need some sleep."

Mary inhaled deeply and let the air out in a big exhale as she gathered her courage to leave him. She picked up her wicker egg basket and left quietly. Fifteen minutes later she returned as quiet as a mouse and Alder was still exactly as she had left him. Cat sat in the rocking chair knitting. "In three minutes, go get my biscuits. I don't want them to burn."

Mary placed the basket on the table and checked the clock. She had a feeling of relief and a sense that everything would be alright.

When Alvin came in at the end of the day, Catherine was still knitting, and Mary was finishing up setting the table.

Alvin rushed to take the plates from her hands. "Should you be doing that? Let me help you."

Mary turned away with the dishes. "Yes, I should, and not until you've washed up. I don't want plates with cow dung on them. You'll make us all sick."

Alvin looked at his hands. They were filthy with dirt and pitch from cutting softwood. "I supposed you're right." Alvin moved to the sink and started pumping the handle. As water flowed, he scrubbed with the tan bar of Fels-Naptha.

"Don't use that. That's laundry soap, use that lye soap."

"This works better for getting pitch off," Alvin protested.

"Well, it'll make your hands raw and cracked. Which reminds me. I need a can of bag balm next time you go to Hemmings."

"I have some in the barn."

"I want my own can, not one you used on cows."

Alvin frowned, "What do you need it for?"

Mary lifted her right breast and lightly jiggled it up and down. "My udders."

Alvin stood staring and confused.

"They can get sore from all the suckling."

He had a moment of understanding and nodded. "I'll get some tomorrow."

They sat down to chicken gravy and biscuits. It was one of Alvin's favorites and he liked the way Catherine made them. She chopped boiled eggs and added them to the gravy which gave it a silky feel when you ate it.

125

Mary had managed a half-dozen bites before Alder began to fuss, and few bites later he started to wail. She got up and sat in the chair to feed.

Catherine turned and looked at Mary. "Learn to feed him and yourself at the same time. Otherwise, you won't have a hot meal for the better part of the next year."

Mary rose and took her place at the table again, clutching Alder close with her left arm and resumed eating.

Alvin smiled and stared at the baby greedily, sucking away.

"What's so funny?" asked Mary.

"Nothing's funny. I'm just enjoying our first dinner as a family. It makes me very happy."

Mary laid down her fork, reached over and squeezed his hand. "It makes me happy too."

Eighteen

Julia sat across from Alvin at her kitchen table. Her hair was in a bun, with loose wisps protruding from the sides. Her eyes were red rimmed and grayish bags hung below eyes one.

Alvin sipped his tea and placed the cup on the table. "Have you slept at all?"

Julia picked at a loose thread on her napkin and shook her head no. "I try. But I am so full of fear, I can't stop my mind. I see nothing but heartache ahead."

"The doctors say Cy will recover. It's just going to take a while."

"You haven't seen him, Alvin. He is wasting away in that cast. Every day the cast looks bigger and every day, he gets a little smaller." A tear started to well up in her eye and she dabbed it with her napkin. The tears were like a cut that continues to ooze and refuses to clot. "I know you said you'll get the harvest in, but how can you do that and get yours in as well?"

"Once when I was in Ireland, I had a little cottage and the roof had collapsed. I didn't have enough men to mend it, but all of my neighbors came, and we accomplished it in a day."

"That was one job. But crops and the day to day running of the farm is more than I can do. Elias suggested we consider selling to the Morelands. He says that when Cy is well again, he can probably get him on at the mill."

Alvin could feel his body becoming stiff at the suggestion and took a long sip of tea before responding. "I can manage the animals on both farms, and we have the McCalls to help. Elias knows better than anyone that any deal with the Morelands is likely to give you just enough to survive and make them richer. I saw the Jones widow and the state Moreland left her in. They went from a farm full of space for their children, to an apartment on the south end of Monroe. All crammed into a space no bigger than your kitchen and front room together. She had been paid something for the farm, but nothing near its full value. I won't let my friends end up like that."

Julia let go of her handkerchief and squeezed Alvin's hand. "When you go to town, will you stop in and see Cy. I think he's considering Elias' offer. I don't want to leave here. I just want my husband back. On our farm."

Alvin squeezed her hand back and nodded. "I will. I'll go tomorrow."

"Thank you."

Alvin sat on his porch watching the sun slowly set behind the barn. The temperature dropped rapidly once the shadows covered the yard. He heard the familiar call of a cardinal and saw a bright red one perched on the top of a bush across the yard, then heard the return call from the female in the lilac tree. He expected the male to come over but was startled when the female took flight and they both disappeared behind the barn.

The bird had been spooked by the sound of a horse and buggy coming up the drive. It was Arthur on his way home from town. Alvin smiled and waved as Arthur pulled the buggy to a stop. He stepped down and made his way to the porch holding a brown ceramic jug and a cloth bag.

"How's my grandson?"

"He's good. A bit young for that, but I wouldn't say no."

Arthur laughed. "I don't imagine you would. This is corn liquor. Pretty potent, but they cut it with water."

"What's in the bag?"

"Soaps and such for the baby and lemons."

"What are the lemons for?"

Arthur held the jug high. "This. You can drink it straight, but it drinks a lot smoother with lemon and a lump of sugar."

"Good to know."

Arthur sat down beside Alvin and lit his pipe. "Have you heard the news?"

Alvin packed his own pipe and lit it as well. "I haven't heard any news."

"The Major is in a bad way. Hasn't been out of bed in a couple of days and refuses to go to the hospital. The doc has been seeing him there, but it sounds like there's no improvement."

"He's too ornery to die."

Arthur chuckled. "Ornery or not. We all die someday and he's pretty long in the tooth."

"Julia Hartley told me that Elias is suggesting selling their farm to the Morelands and when Cy recovers, he might get work at the mill."

Arthur scowled and spat over the porch rail onto the ground. "Did you tell her, don't do it?"

"I did. I said we'd find a way, even if I have to work both farms myself."

Arthur nodded. "Good lad. I won't have Moreland or any of their cronies living on this road if I'm alive." He puffed his pipe. "Do they have any money?"

"I don't know. I get the impression they live season to season."

"As do we all. If they had even a little money, they could probably hire a hand, short of that, maybe they could take in a local lad. Someone say … fourteen or fifteen. There lots of big families on the backside of Howell Hill and if they didn't need to feed one regular, makes their food last longer."

Alvin thought about that for a minute. It made sense to him, they would just need a way to pay him. Room and board was well and good, but if the boy were paid, he'd be more likely to be a good worker and he could help Alvin in the woods between chores.

"Arthur, I think that could work. I don't know how Hartley would feel about a strange boy in his house, but I could ask."

Arthur tapped his pipe out on his heel and sipped it back into his pocket. "Let me ask the boys if they know of anybody they'd trust around their sister."

"Make sure they aren't part of the Walker's collection of imbeciles."

Arthur laughed. "I should hope they'd know better than that, but I'll remind them anyway."

Alvin could see what Julia was talking about. Cy was shrinking inside the heavy plaster cast. He was never a large man, but his once powerful frame has lost the sinewy look as he became more flaccid.

"How's the food?" asked Alvin.

"Tolerable. It's getting use to shitting in a pan that takes some getting use to. Having women wash your ass is a humbling thing."

"Our mothers did it."

Cy winced as he laughed. "I suppose so. But that was a long time ago. Grown men don't want women doing that."

Alvin nodded. "Can't say that I'd want that either." Alvin pulled his chair closer so that no one could hear their conversation. Alvin spoke in something above a whisper. "Have the Morelands been around yet?"

Cy shook his head, no. "I told Elias not to say anything. I don't want to work at the mill."

"Good. Arthur has a plan to help get you through until you're back on your feet."

"What's that?"

"He'll get a local boy from a big family to tend the farm. Do you have a hand's room like we do?"

"We do. What'll it cost?"

"Room and board. I'll be there daily to keep him to his tasks>"

Cy shook his head. "I can't afford any of that. We have enough to pay the bank and taxes, but I couldn't afford a hired hand."

"Don't worry about that. We have a plan for that as well. I'll have him work in the woods with me and I'll pay him out of my end."

"Alvin. You know you're like another brother to me, but I can't be indebted to you, money ruins friendships."

Alvin chuckled quietly. "Do you remember my friend Richard?"

"I do."

"He gave me a cottage and forty acres in Ireland as a gift, because I helped him in the street one day when he was over heated."

"Well, he's a rich lord. It was nothing to him."

Alvin nodded. "You're right. But he did it because I did him a kindness, I'm no lord, but I try to be generous when I can. Someday, I may need a kindness in return for me or my family. Besides, he'll be working for me too, so I wouldn't want him to get lazy."

"I don't know what to say."

Alvin took Cy's and a looked him in the eye. "My brothers are far away. I never see them, only the occasional letter. The McCalls are my brothers now and so are you. Someday we'll sit on your porch and recollect over the times we looked out for each other. That's what brothers do."

"Thank you, Alvin. Help me get through this and I'll show you all the good hunting spots. We'll do our recollecting over drinks and venison."

Alvin gently shook Cy's hand. "I look forward to it."

Cy grimaced as he tried to shift in bed. "I do have one thing that would help me feel better about it."

"What's that?"

"Cut the wood off my land. I've never really cut anything except firewood, so there's an ample variety."

Alvin contemplated on that for a moment. It would mean extra travel for the ponies, but he could start near the tree line and limit the amount of travel in the woods itself, that would make twitching it out that much easier. "I can do that. We'll probably start with getting the rest of your firewood ready. That's give it some time to dry out before the snows fly."

Cy grinned and nodded. "Thank you."

Nineteen

T he McGinns rode toward the Hartley's with Alder swaddled in Mary's arms. In the distance they could see a man on horseback thundering toward them.

Mary held Alder tighter. "What the hell is he about? He'll spook the ponies."

Alvin tightened the reins to keep control of the team. As the rider grew closer he began to slow. It was Winslow Hatch. He slowed to a trot and then to a walk as he approached the wagon.

Mary scowled at Winslow. "Why are you riding so fast. You'll break your neck if that horse falls."

"Have you heard the news? Major Moreland is dead."

Mary crossed herself and shook her head in disbelief.

"We hadn't. Arthur said he was ill, but I figured it'd pass."

Winslow removed his hat in reverence. "Passed in his sleep. I suspect Parker is in charge now. William is away at law school and the others are scattered at private schools. Plus, they're too young. He's the only one that knows the operation over there."

Mary frowned. "Since his wife died, he's worse than his father ever was. The Major was cheap, but people say Parker is mean to boot."

Winslow sighed. "He definitely changed, and not for the better. I figured he'd get better with time."

Alvin forced a grin. "He still might. You never know."

Arthur sipped from a hip flask and slipped it back into his coat pocket. "He was a miserable old son of a whore. Wouldn't have come to my funeral."

Catherine gasped at the statement. "You don't know that Arthur and don't talk ill about the dead."

"What's he going to do about it now?"

"Don't be like that. He was a good man. He fought bravely in the wars."

Arthur pulled his pipe from his pocket and packed it with tobacco. "He was a fighter. I'll give him that."

Catherine scowled. "You'll give him the respect that he deserves. He may not have always been the most pleasant man, but he was just looking out for his family. Same as us."

Arthur lit his pipe and tossed the spent match to the ground. "I hope the son is as reasonable as he was. We may have been competitors, but we dealt in different customers as it were, so we were always able to keep the peace."

The Morelands moved Canadian whiskey throughout Monroe and the neighboring counties. Arthur moved the Poteen to the poor on the west side of Howell Hill and the poorest workers in town. Arthur and the Major had an unspoken understanding, and Arthur never tried to encroach on his customers and Moreland did the same. Alcohol had been illegal in Maine since before the civil war and moonshiners profited. It may not have been legal to drink. But most people did it anyway.

Arthur was lucky and had never been arrested for making the poteen because most of the police wouldn't bother to make the trek up Howell Hill to the Mountain and those that did were usually just looking for a gallon to meet their own needs.

Arthur was puffing his pipe when Kevin and Daniel arrived on the porch, in their Sunday best. They both looked like proper gentlemen and Arthur nodded with approval. Then he stopped and sniffed the air. He scowled and inspected the two boys more carefully.

"What are you wearing?"

The boys looked at each other and replied in unison, "Suits?"

"Not your clothes you simple sons of bitches. Are you wearing perfume?"

Kevin blushed and dropped his head. "It's scented water. The ladies like it."

Arthur took a puff from his pipe and spat on the porch. "Go wash it off. You two smell like you just left a back-alley whore house. What the hell is wrong with you two?"

J.E. MCCARTHY

Catherine frowned. "Arthur, stop it. They are like all the other boys around."

"I don't want them to be like the other boys. I want them to be better. I want them to be men that are respected. Like Moreland. Not everyone liked him, but God dammit they respected him."

The boys went back into the house and emerged a few minutes later with washed faces and hands.

Arthur sniffed at them again and shook his head. "I can still smell it, but maybe it'll wear off in the heat. Go bring the buggy around. You two can sit on the back. It might air you out."

***

Alvin helped Mary up onto the wagon bench and handed Alder up to her. The baby was dressed in a white gown with a lace collar.

"Is that his Christening gown?" asked Alvin.

"It is. It's the nicest thing we have for him. It was mine when I was a baby. Kevin and Daniel wore it too."

Alvin rolled his eyes. "Well, it is hot today. Maybe he'll be cool enough in that." He mounted the wagon, and they waited as they could see the McCalls coming down the road. "We'll let your father lead."

Arthur drove the buggy at a brisk pace and stopped before the driveway. "You lead!" he called out.

"I thought you'd lead us."

Arthur shook his head. "No. I don't want my grandson eating dust on the way and I don't want him to suffer the stink of his aunt's back there."

Alvin chuckled. He could imagine the conversation at the house if the boys were wearing cologne. "My pleasure!" he called back and started down the Howell Hill Road towards the Moreland farm.

The Morelands had a private cemetery a quarter of a mile from their farm. It was only a handful of graves. Malcom's mother, his brothers and their wives, along with Parker's wife. A lilac tree grew on each corner of the lot and Alvin wondered if they had the same number of avian visitors as he did.

They parked the wagon and buggy, a long way up the road. Throngs of people made their way to the graveyard, and no one could get within a quarter mile of it, from all of those coming to pay their respects.

They had arrived a bit early and wanted to find a place in the shade, if possible, but they would have to settle for a parasol instead. Alvin and Mary moved in followed by the McCalls and they staked a spot within sight of the grave.

Alvin jumped when he heard sharp sound of a dozen bagpipes shrilling out the opening notes to Scotland the Brave. A few bars into the song, he heard the rolling beat of snare drums join the pipes and it remined him a bit of Ireland.

The procession of pipers and drummers marched down the road in perfect unison. Followed by the Morelands in a line with Parker at the center holding his mother's hand in the crook of his arm. Alvin watched his face. It was like carved stone, and he stared straight ahead without so much as a twitch. He could see the sweat rolling down Parker's forehead, but he never flinched. He just looked ahead.

Behind them he could see a flag draped coffin being carried by two lines of Army soldiers and being led by an officer holding a calvary saber directly in front of his face as he marched. They too moved in silent perfection. The procession moved into the graveyard and drummers and pipers moved to the back in two long lines. The Morelands sat in chairs beside the grave and the men carrying the coffin stopped while two soldiers removed the flag. They folded it in silence, into a perfect triangle and handed it to the officer that led the March. He moved mechanically and stopped before the Major's wife dropping down on one knee and spoke to her so quietly that no one in the outer crowd could hear what was being said. He rose again and stepped silently to the side.

The service was like so many Alvin had seen in Ireland. He had never seen a Protestant burial, but it looked pretty much the same as a Catholic funeral. When the reverend had finished, the soldiers returned and began to lower the casket into the ground. Alvin jumped again at the sound of a single piper standing apart from the others. The unmistakable sounds of Amazing Grace rang out across the yard and Alvin felt tears forming in his eyes. Maybe it was the pipes. Maybe the moment itself. Whatever it was touched him deep in his heart.

As the song played, the casket disappeared into the ground. The Major was at rest and would stay there for eternity. The pipe when quiet and Alvin said a silent goodbye to the Major. He didn't know him well, but he did like the man.

His prayer for the Major was broken by the sound of shouting. The soldiers had moved into a line to the left of the grave behind the funeral goers. The officer called out command and a rifle volley was fired. Alder began to cry after being startled by the sound. A moment later a second volley and then a third. The Major was gone with all the ceremony befitting a man of his stature.

Twenty

Mary walked with her hand tucked into the crook of Alvin's right arm as he cradled Alder in his left. The processional line to pay respects wound across a line of head stones and up the walking path like long slow snake. She looked ahead and saw a lilac tree that was casting shade on people in line and she felt a wave of envy that those people were getting a reprieve from the sun.

Alvin tilted his body in a way that shielded the baby as he slept. She loved him so deeply. He was as fallible as any other man, but in her eyes, he was still perfect. The line meandered along, and Mary was only a few feet from the shady spot she had longed for. When they made the turn toward Parker and his mother, she saw the pain on his face. She wasn't certain if it was the loss of his father or the burdens of etiquette that were wearing his patience. Those that shook his hand and moved on were met with a polite nod and an almost mechanical move to his next handshake. When someone lingered and wanted to share an anecdote about his father, she saw the internal battle to contain his rage.

She was uncomfortable standing in the shade. Parker and some other men she recognized as his brothers, has been in the sun for hours in dark suits and high collars. Parker was the oldest and his brother William stood next to him. In Mary's mind they were a different as night and day.

Parker was thin and stiff with a stony countenance, sandy hair and thin moustache that gave him a rigid and proper look. William on the other hand was a little shorter than Parker, with a wide frame and dark hair. He had sideburns that rode his jawline and was otherwise clean shaven.

Ahead of them in line was an older man of above average height with white hair and a moustache. Mary noticed his moustache resembled those of a Walrus she had seen in some animal pictures. He must have been in his eighties, but he looked very familiar to her, but she couldn't think of where she had seen him. She thought about people in town and still couldn't place the face. When he turned to the side revealing his profile, she realized who he was and gasped squeezing Alvin's arm.

"Ow." Alvin tried to pull away, but Mary pulled him closer.

"That's Joshua Chamberlain. He was the governor, and he saved the Union in the civil war."

Alvin looked around expecting a man in uniform.

"The man with the white hair talking with William. That's him."

"That man there?" asked Alvin.

"Yes. I'm sure of it. He was a professor at Bowdoin College. He's an amazing man."

"He was a professor and a soldier?"

Mary smiled with pride. "He was."

"I can't fathom that. Most generals I ever heard of were life-long soldiers."

Mary squeezed his arm again. "Can you imagine if we get to meet him? He's probably the most famous person in Maine."

"I'm not sure what he'd have to say to us. I'm possibly the most least famous person from Ireland."

Mary laughed. "Nonsense, you're the most famous person from Ireland I have ever met."

Alvin shook his head and smiled. "I'm the only person from Ireland you've ever met."

"That's not true. I met your brother and father."

"Well. I supposed I could be more famous than them."

The line crawled along until it was their turn to pay respects. Alvin stepped up and shook Parker's hand. "I liked your father. He was a man of character. He will be missed."

Parker looked Alvin in the eye and nodded. "He was that. So, this is your boy? What's his name?"

"Alder. Alder Ambrose McGinn."

Parker studied the child. "Well congratulations to you both. He's a fine boy."

"Thank you."

As they started to pass, Parker reached out and touched Alvin. "Stop by the house after we're done. I want to talk to you."

Alvin looked at Mary and she gave a slight nod. "We will."

Parker released Alvin's arm and turned to William. "Bill. This is Alvin McGinn. The man from Ireland father spoke of."

William's face changed from somber to cordial. "The man who outflanked the Major. Let me shake your hand."

Alvin blushed. "It wasn't like that, to be sure. I just wanted the place, and I had the means."

William smiled. "Relax man. My father liked you. He said if he was going to be outflanked, he was glad it was a man like you."

Mary looked at Alvin and felt a swelling of pride in her chest although Alvin seemed like he might melt at the mention of praise or admiration.

"Thank you. I admired the Major as well."

"I heard Parker invite you to the house afterward. Please come and let's have a drink together in his honor."

"Thank you. I'd like that above all things."

The yard at the Moreland farm was choked with carriages of all styles including several automobiles. Mary was fascinated by the different styles, but one automobile in particular caught her eye.

It was a shiny black two-seater trimmed in copper with bright yellow wheel spokes.

"My God Alvin. Would you look at that? Can you imagine going to town in that contraption?"

"Shhh. You'll make the team cross, and Chum is apt to bite me."

"Well, it would be better than riding around with the rain and snow falling on our heads."

Alvin wiped his brow with a handkerchief and placed it back in his pocket. "It would be nice to get a little shade too."

The house was magnificent. Mary had been by it a thousand times and always wondered what it was like inside. The front door was set back under a balcony supported by massive white columns. Something about it reminded her of pictures she had seen of famous places, like the White House. *How nice it must be to load and unload out of the weather*, she thought.

When she looked around, she didn't recognize many people from town and felt out of place. The women wore dresses she has seen in store windows and the men that weren't in uniform wore suits that looked as if they had been tailored specifically for them.

Mary leaned in and spoke in something above a whisper. "Alvin, why are we here?"

Alvin shrugged. "I don't know. Parker wants to see me, and I don't want to offend him. Besides, it's on our way home anyway."

The lawn was set up with awnings to provide shade and most of the women were gathered under one while the med stood talking under another. Mary felt it getting harder to breathe. "Let's not linger. Alder will want to feed soon and I'm not sure where I could go out of sight. I'm sure people would gasp at seeing me whip a teat out and having him latch on."

Alvin chuckled quietly. "I'm certain they all fed from a teat as some point in their lives. But yes. I'll see what he wants, and we can get back. I need to tend the farms before it's too late."

Mary smiled and squeezed his arm. "Good".

"Ah, McGinns. Over here!" They turned to see William waving them over. Beside him was a small plump woman who couldn't have been much more than twenty. She a curly blond hair that had been put up in a bun.

William shook Alvin's hand. "Alvin, Mary, I'm pleased to introduce my fiancée, Rosemary Waterhouse."

Alvin bowed his head a bit and smiled. "Pleased to meet you. Miss Waterhouse."

"Please. Call me Rose. May I look at the baby. I love babies."

Mary relaxed and handed Alder over to Rose. "Of course. His name is Alder."

Rose beamed as she held him. "He's an angel...and so stout. Come Mary, we have to get him to the shade. You can show him off to the other ladies."

Mary felt the anxiety again, but Rose was so friendly, she was disarmed and felt her lungs relax. "Thank you, Rose. I'd like that." She followed Rose to the awning and the women started fawning over Alder.

William led Alvin to the men's awning where toasts were going round to the Major. A few men had spoken when Joshua Chamberlain rose from his seat with the assistance of a man in uniform.

He cleared his throat and held a glass of water. "When I reflect on the importance on memory and legacy, I say, the power of noble deeds is to be preserved and passed on to the future. Malcolm Moreland was a noble man and a dutiful servant of this great nation. May his deeds be remembered and tales of his example be a model for future generations."

Alvin wasn't what he thought about that toast. He knew that the Major was a good soldier and even though he liked him, in nearly every story he had heard locally, the Major was not to be trusted. In the end, Alvin just accepted that everyone could have their own interpretations and his would be based upon his own experiences.

William tapped Alvin's shoulder. "Let's make our way inside. My brother wants to speak with you."

Twenty–One

William knocked on the heavy wood door that led to the Major's office.

"Enter!" Parker called from behind the door and William turned the ornate brass knob.

The room was a long rectangle completely clad in wood panels from floor to ceiling. A Stone fireplace sat unlit in the center of the right-hand wall, and a set of glass French doors and windows covered the far wall of the room. It reminded Alvin of Richard's den beck in Ireland. A much smaller version, but just as elaborately decorated.

Parker sat behind a massive wooden desk, covered with ledgers and stacks of paper. He didn't bother standing and simply gestured to two heavy wood chairs with leather cushions. "McGinn. Please have a seat. Bill, get him a drink if you would."

Alvin moved to the chair and sat opposite Parker. William poured two whiskeys from a crystal decanter and handed one to

Alvin before sitting. The room made Alvin feel small somehow, and the monstrous desk made him feel even smaller.

Parker closed the ledger he had been working in and folded his hands onto the table. "So, I'm sure you are wondering why I have asked you here?"

"I am curious considering the occasion," said Alvin and sipped his whiskey. It was Canadian and very smooth. If Alvin was being honest with himself, he felt a bit envious that Moreland drank fine whiskeys *off hand* and they settled for homemade hootch and rotgut moonshines when they could get it.

"I'd like to discuss business with you."

Alvin raised his eyebrows in surprise. "Business? Today?"

"Yes. Business. Don't worry, my father is dead, so he won't take offense," Parker said with a light chuckle.

Alvin was shocked at the callousness in which he spoke of the Major.

Parker pointed at William. "He will be our family attorney someday, so I have invited him to stay." Parker pulled a long thin cigar from his coat pocket and lit it. Puffing away as he studied Alvin. "I have a couple of topics. First, liquor. As you probably have heard, we control the importing of liquor in Monroe and the rest of the county for that matter."

Alvin could feel his body beginning to tense, so he sipped his drink again and nodded. "I heard something along those lines."

Parker continued. "Yes, well. It's not exactly a well-kept secret." He leaned forward and used his cigar like a pointer when he spoke to Alvin. "My father and your father-in-law had an agreement. He let McCall peddle that vile Irish piss to the shanties and places where decent people don't frequent. Well, when I say decent, I mean educated, society types."

It suddenly dawned on Alvin that America had a caste system of its own, but without the noble titles. No Earls or Dukes, just haves and have-nots. "I'm familiar with the boundaries of their agreement."

Parker smiled and nodded. "Good. Good. I would like to continue that arrangement but seeing as Arthur McCall is surly by nature and downright hostile when confronted, I thought it best that I work through you. As we are the next generation in this relationship."

"Arthur is his own man; I don't know that he'd listen to me."

"Nonsense man, he'll listen. Just give him wise counsel. I don't even mind if he wants to expand his territory, just as long as the poteen or some homemade brandies don't show up in our restaurants and taverns. Now you can't argue with that."

Alvin thought for a moment. It seemed like a reasonable arrangement and both families continued on with business as usual. "That seems fair."

"It is. Just get word to Arthur that we'll continue on as before and we can both continue to be prosperous."

Alvin sipped his drink again and nodded. "I will."

Parker smiled. "Good man. Now to my second point of business. How is Cy Hartley?"

Alvin felt completely foolish. He should have known that would be Moreland's angle the whole time. He didn't care about Arthur and the poteen; he just wanted to seem civil before he made his real play.

"He's recovering well. Doctors say he's likely to be on his feet by hunting season."

"That's a big stretch between being on your feet and being well enough to run a farm. He might lose everything while he's still in the hospital. I told his brother I'd make him a fair offer, better than the one my father had tried to give him on your place. He could move into town. Everything is close by. Better schools for his children. Mill work is probably easier than farm work and he'd never have to worry about a paycheck."

Alvin scoffed a little under his breath. "Perhaps. But I think Cy likes being a farmer and his own man. What if the mill closes or is destroyed somehow? How would he feed his family then? Farmers are able to provide for themselves."

Parker laughed aloud. "What if he falls off from his roof again? What if all of his animals get sick? You shouldn't work from a position of *what if*. But since we've gone down that road, what if he doesn't pay his mortgage and the bank takes the farm? I'll still get it, just for thirty cents on a dollar of its current value."

Alvin finished his drink and sat the heavy crystal glass on the table with a thud. "He won't default on his loan. I can assure you."

"Really? Would you care to wager?"

"No. I wouldn't want to take your money."

Parker sat back in his chair and studied Alvin. "You are that certain that he'll recover in time?"

"No. I am that certain that he won't default, even if I have to pay it myself."

William looked at Alvin in amazement. "You have that kind of money?"

"I don't. But I could get it if I needed and that's all I'll say about that. But we have enough people to work on his farm until he's well enough to do it himself. There's lots of families on the east side of Howell Hill that have too many mouths to feed. It's one of the pitfalls of being Catholic, large families."

Parker made a courteous grin and nodded his head. "It seems you have it all worked out then. Perhaps I'll look elsewhere for properties."

Parker stood and extended his right hand. "Well, I thank you for your visit. Please feel free to help yourself to food and drinks outside."

Alvin shook his hand and forced a smile. "Thank you, but we need to get back for the afternoon milkings."

"Ah yes, you have two farms to tend now. Better make haste." He pointed at William. "Bill, show him out please and can you find that foul mouthed shopkeeper, Bobbitt if he's still here."

Alvin was about to exit the room when Parker called out again. "Oh. McGinn. Are you still friends with that boxer Armstrong?"

Alvin turned and nodded. "I am."

"Do you know if he's looking for any work?"

"He tends to work his own lots. Why are you looking for someone to cut some wood? There are plenty of fellas on the other side of the hill."

"No, I have no shortage of labor for that. This would be more as a presence to help discourage mischief when I meet with some of these unsavory characters on the Canadian border. They say he's not going to fight anymore; I thought he possibly could use the money. It'd only be a handful of times a year."

Alvin shrugged. "I don't know, but I'll be sure to mention it to him."

"I couldn't ask for more than that. Happy milking."

William led Alvin out and closed the door behind them. "My brother can be a bit of a condescending ass at times." He leaned in and whispered. "Hold your ground on Hartley's farm. We have more land than we can work and that doesn't feed folks in town."

Alvin looked at William in astonishment and wondered how they could be so different.

"Thank you. I will."

"Good. Now let's go see if we can pry your poor son from Rose's grip. She can't wait to have a baby."

Alvin collected Mary and the baby and started the wagon for home. Alvin stared forward without speaking. He was lost in a world of contemplation.

"What did he want?" asked Mary.

Alvin startled back to the present. "He wants Hartley's farm."

"Why? Just to have it?"

Alvin shrugged. "I think so. His brother told me secretly not to let him have it. They won't work it, and we'll have a rotting house down the road in a few years."

"That's it?"

"No. He wants me to inform your father that the old arrangement around liquor is still in place and he'd like to keep things as they are."

Mary laughed. "I doubt Daddy cares much about what Parker Moreland wants."

Alvin sighed. "I suspect not, but it's probably best to keep the peace." It made me uneasy to sit in that room with him. He's an affable enough fellow, but there is something about him that makes me tense. He looks at you like he's searching for a weakness to take advantage of."

Mary scowled. "What makes them like that? Money? How much money do they need? They already have more than they could spend in a lifetime."

Alvin thought about that for a moment. "I don't know. Maybe money and power feed themselves. More money means more power, and with more power comes more money. It's a vicious cycle."

"I'm content with all we have. It's what I imagined as a young girl. I feel like a rich woman."

Alvin reached over and squeezed Mary's hand. "Back in Ireland, a man once told me I was a rich man because of how many friends I had. I think the measure of wealth comes down to what we value most in life. I have you and Alder and the farm. I'm as rich as I'll ever want to be."

Twenty-Two

Arthur sat on a stump across from Alvin smoking a pipe. He had sat in silence for a couple of minutes contemplating on Alvin's conversation with Parker Moreland. He pulled the pipe from his lips and pointed it at Alvin. But before he spoke, he paused and returned to smoking.

The flames felt good as the heat warmed Alvin's face and hands. He was about to light his pipe when Arthur broke the silence. "Dammit!".

The shout startled Alvin and he dropped his pipe in the dirt. As he bent down to pick it up Arthur spat into the flames.

"Allow us to expand our territory? Horse shit. If I want to expand, I don't need his permission and I wasn't afeared of his father and I'll be God damned and go to hell if I'd be afraid of that Nancy boy."

Alvin chuckled. "That's pretty much what Mary said you'd say."

"Well, she knows me. We have a similar disposition." Arthur shifted on the stump and took a long drag from the pipe. "He's up to something. I feel it in my bones. He could sell watered down whiskey to the same folks we sell to. They can't afford the good stuff, and the poteen gets people where they want to go faster. I don't trust him."

Alvin nodded. "The whole conversation made me feel like he was studying me. Maybe to see if I was a Patsy. Couldn't tell."

"Yeah, and this business with Phillip is a ruse too. He doesn't need him for muscle. He probably feels that if Phillip works for him, his loyalties won't be with us. Can't rightfully go against your boss." When he took another drag the pipe was out and he banged it on the heel of his boot then slipped it back into his pocket. "He's a crafty bastard. Just like his old man."

Alvin thought about the Major. He liked him and felt like he was always treated fairly by Moreland. Even more than fairly. "Were you and the Major ever at odds?"

Arthur thought about that for a moment before replying. "I wouldn't call it at odds, but we both had a healthy respect for each other. We both knew of each other's liquor operation and one of us could have turned the other in. But we didn't because we both made money and getting the law involved would have meant the end of both of us. He had money for lawyers, but I had numbers of men that would burn every one of his properties to the ground. I never threatened him with that, but he knew the east side of Howell Hill would revolt against him if anything ever happened to me."

Alvin nodded. "A Pyrrhic victory of sorts."

Arthur scowled. "What the hell does that mean?"

"I read it in a book once. There was a Greek general back in ancient times who defeated the Romans but destroyed his army in the process. His name was Pyrrhus. I guess that's where the name comes from."

Arthur studied Alvin through the flames and smoke, then chuckled. "You're about the most learned farmer I ever met. But yes. I suppose that's what it was. Both of us would have lost and some other amadan would be selling liquor in Monroe."

"Should I tell Phillip about the offer?"

Arthur shrugged. "Go ahead. I wouldn't hold it against him if he went to work for them. Money is money."

"Do you think he will?"

"I doubt it. But not telling him is liable to piss Moreland off and give him a reason to cause us grief."

Now Alvin chuckled. "I don't know. It didn't feel right. Talking with him. That may be a forgone conclusion."

Arthur stood and leaned back, stretching his back. "Well fuck him if he does. I'll be sure he regrets it." Arthur turned from the fire. "I have to piss. Go give that barrel a stir, will you?"

"Of course." Alvin walked to the barrel and lifted the heavy wooden lid and laid it gently on the barrel's side to prevent the bottom getting dirty. On a rack beside the barrel stood a stirrer made from a board that was nailed to a five- foot stick of alder. A thick foam bubble on the top of the mixture and Alvin did his best not to drive the foam to the bottom of the barrel. He could feel the resistance of hundreds of raisins sitting on the bottom. The thing that amazed Alvin about the raisins was that as they sat, they fermented and when they emptied the barrel, the raisins were back to the size of grapes and nearly pure alcohol.

After a few turns with the paddle, Alvin hung it back on the rack and replaced the wooden cover.

Arthur returned to his stump and brought a ceramic jug to his lap and then to his lips. "How's that Merrill boy working out at Hartley's?"

Alvin shook his head and looked at the ground. "Not well. He's a lazy boy. Always off somewhere when you need him and he eats like an animal. It'll be a wonder Hartley's wife and kids don't starve to death feeding him."

Arthur recorked the jug and held it out to Alvin. "I know the lad's father. I could ask him to have a talk with him. Merrills' have a reputation for being hard workers."

Alvin took a swig and handed the jug back. "Well, this one ain't much of one. I can assure you."

"Want me to ask someone else?"

Alvin shook his head. "No. I want to give him a fair chance. Besides, I know other families I can ask. We only need them a short while."

"Suit yourself. Just let me know if you need me. I think I'm going to head inside to bed, be sure to put the fire out. If the yard catches, we'll be blown to bits by the poteen."

Alvin smiled and nodded. "I will. Goodnight Da."

Arthur froze in his tracks and paused. "Good night son."

It was the first time Alvin had called him Da. But now he was as much a father to him as his actual one. Alvin could see that it had meant a lot to Arthur, and he was glad that he said it.

***

September 3rd, 1909 fell on a Friday and with it came the end of summer dance at the Sparta Grange. It was the first time that Mary would be leaving Alder and Alvin could see the tension in her face.

"He'll be fine love. Your mother raised you all without a hitch, I'm sure she can handle a baby for the evening."

Mary sighed. "I know. I just hope he doesn't fuss too much."

"Babies fuss. Your mother will know what to do. It'll give her more reasons to hold her."

Alvin kissed her cheek and Mary slid up close beside him. "What's taking them so long?"

"Probably putting on their perfume. Boy's let's go!" yelled Alvin.

Kevin and Daniel busted through the door in a run and leapt up onto the back of the wagon out of breath.

Mary frowned and plugged her nose. "Jesus. You two stink."

Kevin settled on the second bench behind Alvin. "Don't start. Da just gave us an earful on the way out."

Alvin chuckled. "I'd say you two gave him a nose full, so you're squared."

Daniel plopped down beside Kevin and pulled flask from his pocket. He sipped and offered it to Alvin.

Alvin shook his head. "No. I think I'll wait a bit. Are Winslow and Philip coming?"

Daniel replaced the cover to the tin flask and slipped it into his pocket. "Winslow said they'd meet us there. Phillip was meeting with Parker Moreland today so it's shorter to get to Sparta that way."

Mary scowled and shook her head. "I don't like it. Phillip would never be happy working for that man."

Kaven laughed. "That man? When you were a kid, you never shut up about him and his wife. How beautiful she was. How handsome he had become. Now he's *that* man?"

Mary sat up defiantly. "Well, he changed. When she died, he became mean, and he just looks mad. Not handsome."

"What the hell does he have to be mad about?" asked Daniel. "They have more money than God."

Alvin swatted a bug on the back of his neck and scratched at the bite. "Some things are worth more than money. When you love something more than yourself, you can't put a price on that." He looked at Mary and smiled as if they had a secret language conveyed by looks.

Kevin scoffed at that statement. "Horse shit. Everything has a price, and he's got enough money to pay it."

Alvin shook his head. "You're missing my point. When you love something more than yourself, you cherish it. You protect it and God willing you marry it."

Daniel chuckled from the back. "Hell, at this point, I'd just settle for a kiss."

Twenty-Three

The wagon rumbled on the rutted road jostling the riders from side to side. A few days of rain had made the road soft and wagons as well as the occasional automobile left deep grooves in the earth. When the sun returned it baked the ruts the like clay pots Mary had made as a young girl.

She had been going to festivals and dances at the Grange for as long as she could remember. The Spring Fling on the first Saturday in May, Fourth of July celebrations, countless barn dances and of course the Harvest festivals.

The harvest festivals were always her favorites. The weather was mild, and the sights and smell of fall appealed to her the most. Even more than the spring blooms. The trees were now adorned with gold, red, and orange. There was something about the smell of the leaves that was appealing. When Alvin came home from working in the woods, his clothes had the faint scent of wood and leaves.

As a child, like most children she imagined, they would collect every leaf in the yard and heap them into great mounds, then leap into the air and land on them like some great feather bed. They felt so comfortable that she imagined she could sleep on them.

Her fall bliss was broken by a jolt from the wagon slipping into the valley of a rut that sent her crashing into Alvin and Daniel into Kevin.

Kevin pushed Daniel back to his own side of the bench. "For God's sake Al. Can't you find the road? Danny near crushed me on that last one."

Alvin laughed aloud. "This may be rough but just imagine our trip back in the dark. I won't be able to see them then."

"Well, we'll both be drunk and probably asleep by then, so I won't care."

Mary turned and pointed her finger at her brothers with a scowl. "Daddy said not to let you two get too drunk. He said he needs you two to work tomorrow."

Kavin and Daniel watched her for a moment without speaking. Then Kevin laughed. "My God. She looks just like Ma."

"Oh! She does!" bellowed Daniel laughing. "Did you bring your wooden spoon Mammy?"

Kevin shook his head and smirked, "Don't worry Governess. We'll be ready for work in the morning. Hangover or still drunk. Won't matter. We'll be ready."

"You two are rotten." Mary turned to Alvin. "See how disrespectful they are? Don't let Alder ever at like these two hooligans."

Alvin watched the road. "Oh, I won't love."

Mary looked at him as if he might say more but he just looked ahead with a strained countenance on his face. "Is there something more to say? You look like you want to say something else."

Alvin shook his head and stared at the road.

Mary turned and watched the road with him.

Alvin peeked at her out of the corner of his eye. She sat rigid with her arms crossed. "You did look exactly like your mother though." The three men erupted in a boom of laughter.

Mary flushed and shook her head looking away toward the trees. "You're all rotten."

The Grange Hall was crowded as much as she had ever seen. Wagons were hitched to trees and fence posts as far as the eye could see. They stopped and let wagons pass as those with children left before the crowd became more adult than families.

Pal and Buddy stood watching as other teams passed. Their heads moved in unison as a team of big morgans pulled a wagon full of people back toward Monroe. She wasn't sure if they were watching in admiration or contempt. Buddy stomped the ground twice and snorted as they passed. Pal just drew a deep breath and exhaled with a vibration of his lips.

The sound of an engine could be heard putting in the distance and to Mary's surprise, it wasn't an automobile but more of a gas driven wagon. Two men sat in an open canvas covered cab and three men sat huddled together in the back. The motor wagon had wooden wheels like a wagon and rode much higher than an automobile.

Mary pointed, "What the heck is that contraption?"

"They call it an auto wagon," said Kevin from the back. "That must be from the Moreland farm. They use it to haul grain and such around their properties. Runs on gasoline."

Mary frowned, "It doesn't seem very practical. You can't haul much grain with that."

Kevin shrugged, "I think they still use wagons for big loads, but I suppose it's faster than harnessing up a team for small ones."

Alvin reached over and took Mary's hand. "That's the future, love. Someday we probably won't need horses or ponies at all." He leaned in and whispered pointing at the ponies patiently waiting to work again, "but don't tell them that. They're temperamental enough already."

The auto wagon rumbled by and both ponies pulled back and stomped.

Alvin pulled back on the reins with a slow even tug. "Easy Lads. Easy now." Pal and Buddy relaxed at the sound of his voice.

It had always amazed Mary how quickly Alvin picked up on dealing with animals. When he first arrived, he could barely ride and now just the gentlest word set the beasts at ease. On most days, he still couldn't ride Buddy, but the chestnut pony might pull his own heart out if Alvin called on him to heave a load.

Daniel grew as tired of waiting as the ponies. "We'll jump out here while you tie up," and hoisted himself over the side and only the ground with a great thud.

"We'll see you in there," said Kevin and hopped over the side as well."

Mary could see two men on horseback riding a hundred yards or so behind the auto wagon. It was Phillip and Winslow on their way from the Moreland farm. When they saw the McGinns they quickened their pace and rode toward them.

"Great timing," said Winslow. "We probably would have been here sooner, but that rolling dust storm would have had us covered in dirt from head to toe."

"Is that from the Moreland's?" asked Alvin.

"It is they left a few minutes before we did and we caught up with them a couple miles from here, but it kicked up so much dust we decided to stay back a bit."

"The future doesn't seem any faster than the present," Mary said with a chuckle.

Alvin grinned, "I suppose not, love." He turned to Phillip, "So are you in the employ of the Moreland farm?"

Phillip wiped his mouth and smoothed his mustache. "I am not. It was a reasonable offer. Generous in fact. But I couldn't run my woods operation and work for Moreland too. Besides, to be honest. I don't care for the man. He's got a comeuppance that grates me the wrong way."

Alvin nodded. "I think a lot of folks feel that way."

"Besides, he doesn't need me," Phillip pointed to the back of the auto wagon. He's got that giant half-wit Eustis Oliver working for him."

As the Morland men climbed out of the bed of the wagon, Mary saw a broad shoulders man climb down. He stood well over six feet and when he hopped down from the bed, she saw it pop up about a foot as it was relieved of his massive load. The rest of the Moreland's only stood as tall as his shoulders and at a distance, looked like children standing next to their father.

Alvin shook his head in disbelief. "Christ, that's a big man."

Winslow laughed. "That he is. But he's a bit simple. More beast than man. They use him for the heavy lifting and he's happy just to be fed. No different than Pal there. When we were in school, the kids called him Useless Oliver. He always thought they were just missaying his name and never got the joke."

Mary scowled and shook her head. "Children are so cruel sometimes."

Winslow wiped his brow and adjusted in his saddle, "well, I suspect they heard it from a parent first. Most children aren't clever enough to come up with that on their own."

"Alvin. Don't ever let Alder grow up to be like that."

Alvin laughed, "I won't, love. But you may need to start writing this down. That's two things I need to look out for on this ride alone."

Before he started forward Phillip pulled up closer. "Moreland said to give your father-in-law a message. It's not safe to deal with the LaCroix brothers. He says the police are watching them."

Alvin nodded, "I don't think Arthur cares about the police. He's dealt with them before. But all the same, at least he'll know to be cautious."

Winslow laughed aloud. "Doesn't that strike you as odd, that the biggest bootlegger in the county, knows that the second biggest is being watched? A man might think the police are on Moreland's payroll."

"Regardless of who's paying who. Best to be cautious."

"Thanks Phillip. I'll let him know tomorrow."

Mary playfully punched him in the arm. "Let's get this wagon parked so we can get inside before the party is over."

"Yes, Ma'am." Alvin clicked his tongue and gently snapped the reins.

Buddy and Pal started forward, and Mary thought to herself. *I like the present just the way it is.*

Twenty–Four

The hall was filled with a combination of tobacco smoke and music. The din from the crowd made it so every conversation was something just below a shout and then you still understood about every other word.

Alvin stood on his tiptoes searching for Kenvin and Daniel and spotted Daniel with his arm held high waving from the other side of the hall. He took Mary by the hand and cut a meandering path through the press of bodies until he reached the dance floor.

He quickened his step and led Mary along with Phillip and Winslow to the table.

"Busy place," he said in something akin to a shout.

Kevin smiled and nodded. "We got a table near the window so we can breathe."

Mary tugged on Alvin's arm. "I want to dance."

The dance floor was crowded by at least it offered a bit of space to move. Alvin took her by the hand, and they danced to an Irish reel.

"Did they have dances like this in Ireland?" she asked.

"At weddings mostly. The public house had music, no one really danced, they just stomped their feet to a tune and that was dancing enough."

As if on cue Alvin could feel the floor rumble under his feet. He turned and saw Eustis Oliver dancing with a young woman. She was a plain farmer's daughter with brown eyes and brown hair pulled back in a ponytail. She wore a plain dress that Alvin couldn't help but think she had made herself and brown leather shoes that looked more like a ladies' boot. She looked up at Eustis with a beaming smile of crooked teeth.

Eustis smiled back as he looked down at her. She couldn't have been more than five foot two and he towered over her by more than a foot. Alvin couldn't help but notice his massive hands as they swallowed up her tiny ones. He had the rugged features of a square jaw and large cheek bones covered in a healthy layer of stubble. He danced like an excited child stomping his feet to the time of the music and tilting side to side.

He pulled Mary close to speak without shouting. "Now that's quite a pair. He's so big it looks like he could eat her in one sitting."

Mary peeked around his shoulder and smiled. "That's Norma Bean. She was just ahead of me in school. Her family has a dairy farm to the north of Monroe. She has always been very slight, and the kids used to call her pole bean because she was so skinny."

Alvin shook his head, "More child cruelty. It seems to me that most people out of town are just as poor as one and other."

"They are. I think some kids like to name call because somehow it makes them feel like they are one rung higher on the ladder."

Alvin chuckled. "Where are we on that ladder?"

Mary surveyed the room. "Way higher than most of these people," she said with a laugh.

"Owww!"

The moment of fun was cut by a yowl from the dance floor.

"You stomped on my foot Useless, you gigantic jackass!" It was Emmitt Walker he stood there with a scowl on his face. Alvin found it amusing that his nose still looked puffy and misaligned from where Daniel had broken it on Alvin's first trip to the grange.

Eustis looked at Walker as if he were a child being scolded by his mother. "I'm sorry Emmitt I guess I got carried away."

"You're to big for anything to carry you away and you're shaking the whole dance floor. It's wonder people aren't falling over from the bounce you're causing."

Eustis lowered his head and his smile was gone. "I'm sorry Emmitt."

"You said that already. Watch where you're stepping."

Eustis and Norma continued to dance, gently and the smiles that had once displayed pure joy were replaced with polite grins.

Alvin could see Mary flush with anger. He didn't see her mad very often, but he knew the look. She looked much less like her mother and more like Arthur.

Mary stopped dancing and stood with her hands on her hips. "Geez Emmitt! I'm surprised he didn't step on your nose since it's so damned big now!"

Alvin smiled and groaned. "Oh, sweet baby Jesus."

People stopped dancing and laughed. Emmitt stood blushing and confused, searching for something to say back. People started to return to dancing and Emmitt noticed that Eustis had been one of the people laughing at him. "You think that's funny Useless?"

Eustis stood grinning like a dumb child. "Your nose does look funny. It's different from when we was in school."

Walker stepped forward and shoved Eustis, knocking him back a couple of steps. "I don't want to hear opinions from a half-wit ox like you." He turned and pointed at Mary. "It was her brother what sucker punched me."

Mary leaned forward with her finger pointed at Walker's face. "You were going to sucker punch Alvin and got what you deserved!"

Alvin stepped between Mary and Walker. "Let's everyone just be calm and take break for a minute."

"I am calm," said Mary, glaring past his shoulder at Walker.

"Well then, let's just take a break and get some air by the window."

Mary scowled and turned back toward the table.

Emmitt spat on the floor. "We haven't forgotten about you, McGinn."

"Nor have I about you. So, let's go our separate ways and keep on remembering each other from afar."

The music had stopped and the Walkers along with a few other men moved behind Emmitt, while the four men from the Moreland farm moved to support Eustis.

"That will be far enough gentlemen!"

Alvin heard a voice call from the edge of the crowd. A tall think man with short cropped gray hair pushed his way through the bodies and popped onto the dance floor. He wore a silver badge on his shirt pocket and walked between Emmit and Eustis.

"Dance in peace or leave the floor. Those are your options, Emmitt."

"He stepped on my foot." Emmitt said like a petulant child.

The old man pointed toward the table son the other side of the room. "I don't care if he stepped on your whole damn body. It was an accident, so get moving or I'll help you move."

Emmitt and the Walker cronies dissolved into the crowd. Music started again and the smiles returned to Norma and Eustis.

Alvin turned to Mary. "Who was that man?"

"Hugh MacDonald. They call him Mac. He's the constable."

Alvin had heard Arthur talk about Mac before, but Alvin had pictured a much larger and much younger man. "I'm surprised I haven't seen him before."

"He's retired," said Winslow. "They started hiring him to keep the peace at these events."

Alvin laughed. "Where was he the night Wendell got out of line with Mary?"

"I don't know. Maybe that's why they hired him."

When the evening was done, the partygoers started making their way to wagons and horses. One by one lanterns were lit and hung on wagon parts or just carried by hand from the saddle.

Alvin untied Buddy and Pal while Kevin and Daniel climbed in the back covering themselves with old horse blankets.

Phillip and Winslow untied their horses and were preparing to mount when they heard a voice call from across the yard. "Hey! I heard you retired."

They turned to see Wendell Walker and his collection of idiots walking past to their wagon.

Phillip handed Winslow the reins to his horse. "You talking to me, Walker?"

"Yeah, I heard after you got saved by the bell, you decided to retire from fighting."

Phillip turned and stared at Walker. "Prize fighting."

"Yeah, that's what I said. What are you punch drunk or something?"

Phillip unbuttoned his sleeves and began rolling the cuffs back. "I'm done prize fighting. I'm not going to hurt people for money anymore. Now, I'll do it just to enjoy it."

The smile melted from Walker's face as Phillip started walking toward him. "I'm just ribbing you."

Phillip stopped and sniffed the air. "Oh Jesus. There's that piss smell again. Every time I talk to you, I smell piss. That's the smell of cowardice. You'd better check your pants, Nancy. You might have pissed yourself and don't even realize it."

Walker stiffened and looked behind him. He was backed by his brother and four other men who Phillip recognized as the Hapworth brothers from Palmyra. Six on five. I like those odds.

"Why bring everyone else into it? How about you and I have a go, and then they can carry you home."

Wendell pointed to the wagon. "We got unfinished business with the Irishman and the McCalls."

Phillip scoffed. "Six on five? What kind of a man are you?"

"Six on six," they heard a voice call from the shadows and Eustis Oliver lumbered forward and stood beside Phillip. Alvin found the sight a bit absurd since Oliver was a giant of a man, but Phillip was the one they were all afraid of.

The four Moreland men walked from the shadows as well and now the Hapworths started to get restless.

The oldest one they called Tanner, because he worked at the local tannery pulled at Wendell's shirt. "Let's go. We have a long ride."

Wendell yanked himself free and spun to face Hapworth. "I will not be handled if you don't mind."

Emmitt stepped up beside his brother and pointed a finger straight into Oliver's face. "We stand together, and no one is afraid of you, Useless."

Eustis snatched Emmitt's and squeezed like a python crushing prey. "My name is EUSTIS!" he yelled into Emmitt's face.

Alvin wasn't sure if he heard bone cracking or just imagined it. It was hard to tell what he was hearing over Emmitt's cries.

Eustis forced Emmit to his knees and thrust his arm forward and released the hand, knocking Emmitt to the ground.

Walker writhed in pain on the ground, "he broke my fucking hand!"

Wendell drew his arm back as though he was about to take a swing at Phillip when the night air was spilt by a gunshot. Everyone jumped and turned to see MacDonald walking toward them with a smoking revolver in his right hand pointed in the air.

"You've gone just about far enough Mr. Walker. So, unless you'd like to spend the next few nights in the county jail, I suggest the six of you get in that wagon and get headed for Palmyra." He turned to the McGinns and Morelands. "And you get headed back to Monroe or you'll find yourselves there with him." He holstered his gun and took out a pack of cigarettes and lit one. "Walkers first. Then I'll let the rest of you go, that way there's no chance of an *accidental* meet up."

The Walkers left without incident and Moreland's did as well. But before they left Phillip reached out to shake Oliver's hand. "Strong grip. If you ever find yourself in need of work, come find me. I work hardwoods mostly, but you know what they say?"

Eustis shook his head. "I don't."

"Hard wood makes hard men."

Twenty–Five

M ary cuddled Alder close to her chest while drifting between dreams and waking in those last moments of a good night's sleep. The room itself felt chilly, but she and the baby were comfortable in their little shelter under the heavy quilt. It was a quilt she had made as a girl and had been stored in a cedar hope chest Arthur had made for her twelfth birthday. It had only been a few years since that birthday, but in her mind, it was long, long ago.

The past year had been a whirlwind to her. She became pregnant and got married. Not in the traditional order of life, but she didn't care. She knew that she wanted Alvin from the moment she met him and now he was hers, along with the gift of this beautiful boy.

She slid out of bed and covered him gently with the edge of the quilt, while she dressed. The sun was just rising and a beam of light rested on her face. She squinted at first but then just let the sunlight wash over her face. When she opened her eyes again,

Alvin was walking from the barn with a pail of milk in one hand and a basket in the other.

She picked up Alder and brought him to her chest slowly so as not to wake him yet and made her way downstairs. She could feel the heat of the woodstove on the stairs, and it felt wonderful.

Mary reached into the basinet and the blanket that served as a mattress felt comfortably warm, so she laid Alder there to finish sleeping.

Alvin came through the door from the summer kitchen as quiet as a mouse and smiled to see Mary's face.

"Good morning, Love."

"Good morning, husband," Mary said with a giggle. It still seemed so new to her and hadn't lost its luster yet. "You're up early today."

Alvin placed the pail on the floor and the basket of eggs on the table. "I want to get down to Cy's early to that shiftless farmhand Merrill to work early today. We need to get the smokehouse ready to slaughter Cy's hogs and we need to pick his apples before they all fall on the ground and get eaten by deer."

"Are you leaving instantly?"

"No. Not until after breakfast, why?"

"I want to come with you. I have a bag of fabric scraps and Julia, and I are making quilts. They'll be handy come December."

"Of course, Love. It's going to be a nice morning for a ride."

October was always a funny month in Maine. The mornings started out chilly, sometimes with frost and as the day wore on it became comfortably warm without getting too hot. Her father always said it was the best month to get work done on the farmhouse itself.

The ride was nice, and Alder only fussed for a moment when the cool air hit his face. His eyes popped open, and he drew a deep breath then cried with the shock. But as the wagon rumbled down Howell Hill Road he calmed and looked around with his little eyes, taking in the gigantic new world.

Hartley's farm was a nearly identical match to their own, so it seemed funny in Mary's mind whenever she visited. It was like the same house, but everything was out of place.

"Dammit," said Alvin.

"What's wrong?"

"He barely split any wood yesterday. We sawed a cord of wood in the morning, and he only split about two dozen pieces."

"Maybe he was busy with something else," Mary said trying to soften Alvin's mood.

"I hope so. They have a good amount of wood already, but Arthur says there's nothing worse than trying to pick wood out of the snow, when it could have been split when the weather was still good."

Mary laughed. "He knows from experience. There's been more than one winter where he was still splitting wood in January."

When the wagon came to a stop, Albert Merrill was sitting on a bench in the barn wrapping the neck of the maul with a piece of leather. Alvin locked the wagon and helped Mary and Alder down before confronting Merrill.

"What are you doing," he called across the yard. "Is the handle broken?"

Merrill looked up with a frown at being questioned, "no, it hurts my hands when I overswing, so I'm adding some padding."

Mary could see Alvin's whole-body tense as he tried to contain his anger. "I'm going inside. I'll see you at lunchtime."

He marched forward toward the barn as if he hadn't even heard her, then raised a hand to wave, but never looked back.

Mary watched as he walked away and thought, *I wouldn't want to be Merrill this morning.*

Mary and Julia sat sewing squares of cloth while the Hartley children played on the large, braided rug that nearly filled the living room and Alder laid on his back clutching a silver rattle Richard had sent as a gift from a silversmith in London.

"I think Alvin might throttle Merrill today," Mary said with a chuckle.

"Good. I hope he does," Julia said without looking up from her work.

"Why? What has he done now?"

"It's not bad enough that he's lazy and eats more than even Cy ever did, but I think he's a pervert."

Mary placed her sewing in her lap and studied Julia. She looked upset and was unusually quiet today. "What happened?"

"I'm embarrassed to talk about it."

"Tell me. Did he touch you?"

"I don't know what he's about. Last evening, I had heated some water on the stove to bathe and took the basin to my room. He was already in the hand's room, and I thought that he had gone to bed. When I was undressed and bent over washing, I heard a creaking of the floorboards, and I jumped and covered myself and it stopped. When I started to wash again, I heard the sound a second time. Then I realized I was washing in front of the door, and the sound was coming from outside the door. So, I moved to the dresser and put on a nightgown. All the time I could hear the floorboards creaking back toward his room. I think he was watching me bathe through the keyhole."

"Oh my God. I am so sorry Julia."

"Cy is the only man to ever see me naked, except for the doctor who delivered our babies. It's private. For my husband. Not that vile worm."

"We need to tell Alvin."

Julia wiped away the tears that had started to form in her eyes. "This morning, he kept staring at my breasts and looked like a hungry little dog. When he was done breakfast, I was at the sink and he brought his plate over, which he never does and ass he passed he brushed his hand across my backside."

"What?" Mary was in utter shock.

"He immediately apologized and said it was an accident. But he never brings his plate to the sink, he just leaves it like I'm the maid rather than his employer."

Mary became flushed with anger. "We're telling Alvin, now."

"There's so much work to do and Cy will be coming home soon."

Mary reached over and took Julia's hand. "Alvin is clever. He'll figure it out even if we have to bring one of my brothers to help. Albert Merrill isn't spending another night here. He's a bad egg."

"I believe you. I just don't want more hassles for Alvin after all he's done for us."

Mary shook her head, still angry from hearing the story and tried to imagine what Alvin would do to a man if that had been her, or even worse what would her father have done. They might never find that pervert Merrill if he had peeped on her.

"Alvin will know what to do. If not, my father will."

Mary stepped onto the porch and Alvin was splitting the wood while Merrill loaded it into a wheelbarrow. She couldn't even stand the sight of him. She had grown up around tough boys all her life, but he wasn't one of them.

Alvin swung the big maul and the stick of wood exploded in half; he picked up one of the halves and split it again. She could tell by the ferocity of his swings that he was still angry.

Good, she thought. This will be the straw that breaks the camel's back.

"Alvin!"

Alvin stopped and turned.

"I need you for a minute."

Alvin handed the maul to Merrill. "Keep going I'll be back in a minute." As Alvin walked to the porch, Merrill took the maul and swung it with so little power that it immediately became wedged in the stick of wood.

He's a bad egg and a useless one, she thought.

Alvin stepped onto the porch. "What is it, Love?"

Mary took him by the hand. "We'll need to step inside. Julia has something to tell you."

Twenty–Six

The farmhand's room at the Hartley farm was much more spartan than the one at his own house. A twin sized bed lay against the left wall and a small table sat next to it. Although the room had a trunk for clothes, Merrill kept two piles on the floor. One that looked to be clean and one that was clearly soiled.

A farmhand's life was a spartan existence, so the room was all that was really needed. Merrill likely only owned three pairs of pants and a similar number of shirts. Alvin opened the trunk to find a canvas bag that Merrill had used to bring his clothes and few belongings. Alvin picked up the bag and found two tattered photos hiding underneath it.

One was of a woman topless wearing a cloth around her waist and the other one was of the same woman holding the cloth to her front while her bare backside was exposed. His first impulse was to tear them up, but they belonged to Merrill and felt it wasn't his place. He dropped the photographs into the bag and stuffed his clothing on top of the photos.

A lamp and matches were the only things on the little table and Alvin looked under the bed. A ceramic jug was hidden there. Alvin slid the jug from under the bed and pulled the cork. It was apple cider beginning to ferment.

If he's hiding this, what else is he hiding? Thought Alvin. Alvin searched the pillowcase and bedding and found nothing else. When he lifted the mattress, he saw a flat packet wrapped in cloth and picked it up to review the contents.

Alvin stared in disbelief, then tossed the packet onto the bed. It was a pipe and a leather tobacco pouch that Alvin had seen with Cy half a hundred times. A silver pocket watch with the initials C.B.H. engraved on the back and most disturbingly, a pair of ladies' silk undergarments.

Alvin stuffed the underclothes into his pocket. It was bad enough that Merrill had stolen her dignity, but Alvin would not be able to tell her the whole truth. He picked up the back and the packet walked downstairs. Julia was making some food for her children and Mary was feeding Alder.

"Do you have all his things?" asked Mary.

"I do, and a bit more." Alvin laid the packet on the table, unfolding the cloth to show the pipe, tobacco pouch and the watch.

Julia gasped. "Those are Cy's things. He's been in out bedroom."

Mary scowled. "Oh my God. Was there anything else?"

"Just a jug of cider he's been hardening under the bed. I'll go take care of that after I take care of him."

Julia picked up the watch. "Should we contact the police?"

Alvin shook his head. "No. I don't think so. He had them hidden away, but they are still on the property. Let's just get him moved on and that should be the last of him."

Julia's face flushed and she held the watch to her heart. "Just get him away from here. Far away."

Alvin picked up Merrill's bag and stepped out onto the porch. The maul was leaned against the large piece of log that they had been using for a chopping block, but Merrill was nowhere around. Alvin placed the bag in the back of the wagon and walked to the barn.

Merrill was sitting against the wall with his feet crossed chomping on an apple.

"What are you doing?"

Merrill held up the apple and spoke through a mouth full of food. "Taking a break, chopping wood is hungry work."

"It is indeed. Well hop up, we need to go to Hemmings to get grain and some other supplies."

Merrill jumped to his feet. He was thin with greasy brown hair and blue eyes that seemed to set too far back. His face reminded Alvin of so many rats he had seen in his life. Merrill jumped up on the bench and Alvin unhooked the team. Alvin climbed up and Merrill had the reins in his hands. "Can I drive?"

Alvin reached over and took the reins from Merrill. "No. I prefer to be the one to drive my team."

"Okay."

The wagon turned and started up toward his farm.

Merrill looked up the road, the other way. "Hey, you're going the long way."

"I know. I have a stop to make this way."

They rode along in silence for a bit. Alvin didn't want to even look at him. He just cast his gaze on the road ahead while the wagon rumbles along.

Merrill began to fidget and was uncomfortable with the silence.

"Do you think we'll slaughter the hogs this week? Pork's a good meal."

"I have other things to do first."

They passed his own farm and rolled along until they reached the McCalls. Alvin yanked the brake and jumped down. Merrill was starting to dismount when Alvin held up a hand. "Wait here. I'll just be a minute."

Alvin went to the porch and knocked on the door. Arthur answered and Merrill could see them speaking. Arthur stuck his head back in the door and Daniel appeared. He and Alvin returned to the wagon and Daniel climbed in back while Alvin remounted.

They rode along, making small talk, mostly between Alvin and Daniel. Merrill tried to join the conversation, but he only received curt answers in return.

"Do you think we'll get a chance to hunt soon?"

"Probably."

"Have you seen many deer near your apple trees?"

"Some."

"Think we'll have a hard winter?"

"Don't know."

After a while, Merrill stopped asking questions and just listened.

When they pulled up to Brownfield Road on the far side of Howell Hill, Alvin stopped the wagon and reached into his pocket, pulling out a handful of change. He handed it to Merrill. "Here."

Merrill looked at the coins trying to comprehend why Alvin would be giving him money.

Alvin reached behind the bench and picked up the bag with Merrill's belongings and laid it on the bench between them.

"Your services are no longer needed. There's a dollar and four bits there. Give it to your mother. I wouldn't spend it on yourself, because I'll ask your father about it the next time, I see him and you can deal with his wrath."

Merrill looked at Alvin as befuddled as if he had just woken up, "Why?"

Alvin scratched his chin. "I'm not sure where to start. Maybe with this." Alvin reached into his pocket and pulled out the silk undergarment. "This was hidden under your mattress along with some items belonging to my friend Cy. Including a silver watch given to him by his father."

"I found those things and forgot to bring them back, so I..."

Alvin cleared his throat. "You're a liar now. As well as a thief and possibly a pervert."

Merrill flushed and opened the bag and rummaging through the clothes. "I had personal things in that trunk too."

"The photographs are in there."

"Looking at pictures of naked girls don't make you a pervert."

"You're right. They probably don't. But peeping through a keyhole at a woman just trying to wash does."

Merrill sat back red faced and looking as guilty as a child with a hand in the cookie jar. "That never happened. I thought I heard something, so I walked to the top of the stairs and when I saw things were okay, I went back to my room."

Alvin shook his head. "It's funny how you knew the exact time I was speaking of without having to ask. It could have been days ago. But you knew I was talking about last night."

Merrill realized he was caught and dropped his head. "What are you going to say to my father?"

"I should go down there and lay the whole story out for him. But I won't. He's a respected man and your mother is a god-fearing woman. I don't want the sins of the son to smear their name."

"I appreciate that," Merrill mumbled.

"Tell them we don't need a hand anymore since the harvest is in and the dollar-fifty is money you saved, they'll be proud of you, even if you really are a liar and a thief. Let them believe their son is good. At least until you get caught again."

Merrill frowned and looked Alvin in the eye. "You're not better than me."

"Probably not. But I'm not a thief." Alvin turned to Daniel and motioned with his head for Daniel to get out. Daniel stood and hopped over the side. Alvin took Merrill's bag and tossed it on the ground.

Daniel moved to the side where Merrill was sitting. "Get down boy."

Merrill looked at Alvin then Daniel. "I'm going." He climbed down and yanked his bag from the dirt and stood defiantly glaring at them.

Daniel stepped forward and put his hand on Merrill's shoulder, then grabbed Merrill by the crotch of his trousers and squeezed.

Merrill squealed like a piglet and Daniel whispered into his ear. The conversation took no more than ten seconds, but Merrill's face was so contorted, Alvin thought it might burst.

Daniel let go and shoved Merrill to the ground, where he rolled in the dirt, writhing in pain.

Daniel climbed up beside Alvin and they rode away. When Alvin looked back Merrill was just getting to his feet and picked up the bag doubled over in pain. He just started dragging himself up the road to home.

"What'd you say to him." asked Alvin.

"I told him to stay away from all our properties and if I ever see him there or hear he's said something foul against us, I'll rip his balls off for real."

"That'd be warning enough for me."

"Let's hope he heard me through all of his squealing."

Twenty–Seven

T he day Cy came home from the hospital was cold and damp. It wasn't rainy, but Mary could feel the chill to her core. As long as her feet were cold, it felt impossible to get the rest of her body warm.

She and Alder spent the morning with Julia and the children while Alvin rode to town in a covered buggy he borrowed from a neighbor.

They had packed extra blankets into a bag and filled a basket with meat, cheese and bread. They even filled a thermos with hot coffee for the men to share on the way home.

The doctors had removed Cy's cast two weeks before and had spent the time helping him to walk and get himself to and from a sitting position. It seemed like it would be a natural thing to walk again, but the weeks in the cast had caused his muscles to shrink so that he looked more skeleton than man.

The house looked pristine, and the children bathed and wore their Sunday clothes for the occasion. George was three and dressed in pants and a shirt with a navy jacket. Grace was two and Julia had dressed her in a velvet dress that seemed to change colors in different light. They both had straw colored hair and light blue eyes like Cy.

"George really looks like Cy, doesn't he?"

Julia smiled. "He does. Just as stubborn as Cy too."

Mary watched her admiring the children. "You must be ready to jump out of your skin with excitement."

"I am. But I am so nervous. What if he falls or something and has to go back?"

Mary moved closer and reached out for her hand. "He's not going to fall. We'll be here to help until he's fully back on his feet. If there's a setback, we'll still be here. Alvin likes Cy a lot and I think he likes having a friend that's a man and not a relation. My brothers are still teenagers, and Alvin likes to be around men his own age."

Julia squeezed her hand and smiled. "Well, I know Cy thinks the world of him as well. He keeps talking about going hunting with Alvin."

"I hope they go. There's nothing like fresh venison. My father is obsessed with cooking the perfect quarter of a deer. He says he's come close a few times but still hasn't quite reached perfection."

Julia looked out the window to inspect the road for the carriage. "Do you think it's warm enough in here. The kitchen is nice, but I wonder if we should start a fire in the living room."

Mary smiled, "I'm sure it's fine, but if you want to start one, there's nothing like a hot stove to help you relax. I'll go get some wood if you want to start on the kindling."

"Thank you. I will."

Mary went to the shed that adjoined to the summer kitchen and loaded an armful of wood. When she returned, Julia had already lit the stove and added some small pieces of hardwood to the little fire.

The fire snapped and crackled as flames wrapped the wood like fingers tightening their embrace. Mary stacked the wood in a metal holder that kept the wood from falling onto the floor. Julia closed the front, and they could already feel heat radiating from the ornate parlor stove. I was a black iron cylinder with steel trim work and four small windows on the door.

They both stood admiring their work when the unmistakable sound of a carriage could be heard in front of the house. Julia rushed to the window and squeaked with delight. "He's home. Children, daddy is home."

George dropped the wooden train he had been playing with and ran to the door. He reached up with both hands trying to turn the knob. "Mama, help."

Julia picked up Grace and moved to the door. "Come on, George. Let's stand back and give him a minute to come in."

George stood by his mother as restlessly as a team of ponies at the fair, waiting for the word to go.

Footsteps could be heard on the steps, slow footsteps and then they could see his face in the window.

George jumped in place with excitement, "Daddy."

The door opened and Cy stood in the doorway with Alvin at his side in case he lost balance.

Cy stepped into the house and George charged like a tiny bull and flung his arms around Cy's legs. "My daddy."

Grace was reaching out for Cy and Julia moved to meet him. "Georgie. Let Daddy get inside out of the cold."

Cy leaned in and kissed Grace and then Julia on the cheek and she jumped.

"Ooo. You really are cold. Come stand by the fire and take the chill off."

He had a cane but was moving quite well without it.

"Are you in much pain," asked Julia.

Cy held his hands over the fire and shrugged. "I feel more stiff and weak, than actual pain. It's worse in the morning when I get out of bed, but as the day goes on, I get around well enough."

Julia wrapped her arms around him and laid her head on his shoulder. "I'm so happy to have you home. Promise you'll never leave us again."

Cy thought about protesting the absurdity of a promise like that, but instead he turned and kissed her again. "I promise."

Alvin brought Mary and Alder back to the farm before leaving again to return the carriage. As they rode, she watched him and felt proud of all he had done for the Hartleys. There was still more to do, but seeing Cy in his own home felt like a milestone to her.

He seemed to sense her stare from the corner of his eye and peeked over to see her grinning at him.

"What are you doing?"

"Admiring you."

"Why, because I'm so good looking?"

Mary laughed. "Oh God no. You have middling looks at best. No because I am proud to have a husband like you. Most of the men around here would have encouraged the sale to Moreland to curry favor. But you saved your friend's farm."

"I'm sure he would have done the same for me."

"Probably. But I'm proud all the same."

"Thank you, Love. You deserve half the credit. I think Julia would have been lost without you."

Alvin looked up the road to their farm and saw a cardinal sitting on the mailbox and started whistling his cardinal call.

The sharp sound woke Alder, and he began to fuss.

Mary poked Alvin in the side. "Stop that noise, he doesn't like it."

"Sorry. Have you checked the post lately?"

"What post?"

Alvin chuckled. "The mail."

"Oh. No, I haven't, I've been so busy with Julia I hadn't thought to look. I don't think it came today, we've been watching the road waiting for you.'

"If I pull up close, can you check the box?"

"Of course." Mary shifted Alder to her left arm and slid to the seat edge as Alvin pulled up to the box. She opened it to see a solitary letter. "We have a letter." She pulled it from the box and closed the door. When she flipped the envelope over, she could see it was from Ireland. "It's a letter from your mother."

Alvin beamed. "Glorious. Let's get settled and read it over some tea."

Mary poured tea for them both and brought out a little jar of honey and a tin of cream. Alvin took his tea black and sipped while she made hers the way she liked.

"Are you going to open it, or just admired the handwriting?"

He chuckled. "I'm waiting for you to be settled."

"I'm settled."

"Good. I'll begin."

The letter was several pages long and provided updates on everything in the village. It was the last page that caught them off guard. Annie asked if it would be a good time for Jameson to join them in America. Troubles between the Irish and the English were starting to become volatile, and she wanted him far away to either Canada or America. Since Alvin and Mary had a farm, she thought that would be the best place.

Alvin laid the letter on the table. "What do you think?"

"About what?"

"Jameson moving here."

"Alvin. I wish your whole family would move here. Of course he's welcome. Look how much room we have. We don't even use three of the bedrooms upstairs, I'm sure he'll love it."

Alvin smiled. "I'm so happy to hear that. I knew that would be your answer, but I never want to do something so big without us being in agreement."

Mary held his hand and leaned across the table to give him a kiss. When she sat back she chuckled softly, "Too bad he hadn't come a couple months ago, we wouldn't have had to deal with that worm, Merrill."

Twenty-Eight

Alvin had gone to town to send word back to Ireland that Jameson was welcome to come anytime and the sooner the better to prevent being caught by winter. He sent the message by telegraph instead of mail to save on time. It cost a dollar fifty to send the message, which was outrageous compared to the five-cent cost of a letter, but it was better than waiting weeks and running the risk of it getting lost or finding its way to the bottom of the Atlantic in a storm.

After sending his telegram, he met with Omar LaCroix at a little Diner on the outskirts of Monroe and relayed the story about the police watching them.

"The police won't bother me. They're some of my best customers. But to be safe, we'll meet in the woodlot down at the lower mill. It's a long way for the police to ride and if you come around noon, they'll be off to lunch, and you can be home for dinner."

The plan made sense to Alvin although meeting out of town would have seemed to be a safer option.

Arthur handed ceramic jugs to Alvin, and he packed them under the bench seat of the wagon wrapping each one in cloth to prevent too much rattling. When the seat was packed, he jumped down to get his final instructions.

Arthur always tried to plan for contingencies and Alvin was starting to pick up the practice himself. "I'm going to bring an extra gallon in case I'm stopped by the police. I'm hoping a gallon would be enough to have them look the other way."

"I suspect it would," said Arthur. "I'm going to send Kevin with you, and here, take these. Arthur walked to the porch and returned with two long, straight, maul handles. "I need these back, so try not to break em'. But if you do, be sure to break the man you hit with it."

Alvin assessed the weight in his hands as he placed the staves behind the bench and smiled. "Let's hope our wits are enough to get us back in one piece. But if not, those will leave em something to remember."

"I'd send Daniel, but he's down to Hartley's and his red hair and size attracts attention. Better to be unseen on a trip like this."

Arthur turned toward the porch and scowled. "For the love of Christ Nancy! Will you move your arse!"

Kevin stepped onto the porch wearing a coat and a Derby hat set at a slight tilt and strode forward to the wagon. He looked to Alvin like a man now and not so much a boy. He had brown hair and blue eyes like his mother and a solid frame like Arthur. Although Kevin looked to be a couple of inches taller.

Arthur pulled his pipe for his pocket and shook his head as he packed it. "Good God man. You're dressed like a Dandy."

Kevin climbed aboard the wagon. "I'm dressed for business."

Arthur eyed his son as he lit his pipe. "I suppose you are. But be sure you remember what type of business you're about. In the liquor business, you need be sure you're smart, not just look smart."

Keving straightened his jacket and opened the left side. A leather bag full of sand on a thong, hung from a button on the jacket lining. "Just in case."

Arthur smiled. "Good lad. There may just be hope for you yet."

The ride to town was the same as every other ride they had taken, but it somehow felt different to Alvin. There was tension in his body and his mind raced through every possible manner of chaos they might encounter.

The sun was shining, but the air was cold and slipped into any opening in Alvin's coat, no matter how slight, to send an icy tendril around his neck and down his back causing him the occasional shiver. He pulled his collar up tight and hunched on the bench to conserve as much heat as he could.

He was lost in a thought when he jumped at Kevin, breaking the silence. "Think Hartley will make a full recovery?"

"I do. He's a strong man."

"He is. I'm glad he didn't sell to Moreland. Da might have burned the farm down. He's talked about nothing else and I'm not sure my mother can take much more of his ranting."

Alvin chuckled. "I'd think she'd be used to it by now."

"Danny and I ignore him. But we don't have to sleep with him. She's got no chance to get away."

"Well, she can always come to my place. I know how she dotes on that baby."

Kevin adjusted his hat and buttoned the top button of his coat. "He hated them you know."

"Who the Morelands?"

"Yes. In his mind, they are no different than Richard's father. So, he relishes any chance to take them down a peg."

Alvin handed Kevin the reins and rooted around in his pocket to fetch his pipe. He turned toward the back of the wagon to block the wind and lit up. Then took the reins back. "I'll tell you what I believe. The Moreland's wouldn't spend five minutes worrying about us unless we give them a reason to. They've always been civil with me. Perhaps they just want to irritate your father. But I have found that with rich people, petty squabbles and always secondary to business. They have a liquor trade; we have a liquor trade. It serves us both better if we can coexist without fighting. There's no money in it."

"How do you know that?"

"History." Alvin puffed his pipe and blew the smoke into a cloud above his head. "The Romans didn't allow fighting. Once the conquered a people, they worked with them to keep the peace. They needed the resources to be sent back to Rome and fighting disrupts the flow of those resources. It's bad for business."

Kevin scratched at a patch of hair sprouting from his chin. "How do you know all that? Did they teach you in school?"

Alvin laughed. "God no. We learned to read, write, and perform mathematics. But mostly we learned Catholicism. The rest I learned from reading books."

Kevin laughed aloud. "I read Huckleberry Finn once and convinced Danny that we should build a raft to ride down the brook to see where it went.'

"Did it float?"

"It did on its own, but once we got on board, our weight was too much, and it sank. The problem was that it was during the spring runoff, and the water was something just a shade above being frozen."

Alvin shuddered at the thought. "That sounds rather unpleasant."

"It was. When it sunk, we jumped off and waded to shore to get dried off and the damned raft popped up from the bottom and floated down stream. That next summer, I was fishing at

Patten Pond up the road from the farm and I saw the raft hung up in the march with pussy willows growing up through it. Damned thing made it to the pond. It would have been a hell of a ride."

Alvin laughed. "I know that pond. It must be half a mile, maybe more."

"It is. About that anyway. At least it was seaworthy," Kevin said with a smile. "Foolish kid stuff I guess."

Alvin knocked the spent tobacco from his pipe and slid it back into his pocket. "Nonsense. That's the beauty of books. It feeds the imagination. I remember the first time I read Treasure Island. I wanted to hop on a ship and find a buried treasure. I even buried a wooden box full of trinkets and made a map. When I went back to it, the box had rotted through from all of the rain, but there was still a thrill from having found it again. I thought about that box when Kellen and I boarded the ship to Canada. You never know what adventures you'll find until you look."

They rode along the edge of Monroe and made their way to the lower mill yard. Along the way they passed a policeman on foot heading in the opposite direction. On his way to lunch no doubt, thought Alvin. I guess Omar was right.

The lower mill yard sat on the bank of the Black River down a long steep hill. Alvin was forced to keep tension on the reins to prevent the ponies from gaining too much speed as they made their descent. When they reached the bottom, Omar and Rene sat next to three horses eating bread and cheese from a cloth laying on a block of wood.

Omar looked up and smiled. "Bonjour, McGinn. Any trouble getting here?"

Alvin locked the brake and jumped down from the bench. "No but we passed the police on the way here. How long is his lunch?"

"It's a long lunch today. He's been paid and the tavern is on the way to the station," Omar said with a loud laugh.

Alvin smiled and tapped on the bench. "I have a bit of something to wash down your bread."

Twenty-Nine

M ary laid Alder down in the crib that Alvin had made and stroked his head with the lightest touch. He was milky white, and his head was crowned with medium brown hair. It had grown beyond the wisps at birth to something that could be smoothed over his bald little head.

She stroked his cheek with the back of her fingers and tried to recall whether she had ever felt anything so soft against her skin. She couldn't recall anything. Mary smiled and leaned in kissing his forehead.

When she rose, she could hear the rumble of a wagon and looked out to see Alvin with Kevin and a giant man all crammed onto the wagon bench. It was Eustis Oliver and her husband and brother looked something akin to children sitting on each side of him. She slipped over on tiptoes to the door and wrapped her shoulders in a blanket to guard against the cold.

Mary stepped onto the porch and shuddered against the chill. Something was wrong. The men weren't speaking, and Kevin's lip was swollen and bloody. Alvin pulled the break and jumped down without so much as a hello.

"What's wrong?" she asked.

"Nothing love, we'll be in directly. Let me get the ponies put away."

Kevin climbed down and Eustis followed. The wagon sprung up a half a foot when he dismounted and he helped Kevin to the porch.

Mary stepped forward and took Kevin's hand. "My God. You're hurt. Are you okay."

Kevin touched his swollen lip and winced. "Gave better than we got."

Alvin sat with a cup of tea in his hand still trying to warm up from the ride back from town. "It was the Morelands." He looked at Eustis. "If it wasn't for this lad, we'd probably still be waking up on the street."

Mary's chest felt tight, and she struggled to take a breath. "Why? What happened? I thought you said Moreland was okay with you selling in town."

"He did. Maybe he changed his mind. It was the LaCroix brothers they were after, we just happened to be there at the wrong time."

"I don't understand any of this? They attacked you?"

Alvin nodded. "They did. They showed up just after we were paid by the LaCroix's. They had that auto wagon and there were five of them. Hammond, the foreman said the LaCroix can't sell liquor in town anymore and Omar told him to go feck his mother." Alvin sipped the tea and placed the cup on the table. "Hammond took offense to that and challenged him to a fight. Omar obliged and when he started to knock the piss out of Hammond, the others jumped in, then so did we. That's when Kevin took a blow to his lip."

Kevin scowled. "One of those sneaky sons of bitches caught me from behind."

"Rene jumped in and when the fight more of less stopped, Hammond started to berate Eustis for not getting involved and told him to break Omar's arm."

"I'm no animal," Eustis mumbled. "I wouldn't want to hurt a man."

Alvin patted Eustis on the shoulder. "You're not. You're a good man."

"They called me Useless."

"They did," said Alvin, "and they were wrong."

Mary surveyed the three men in shock. "How did they leave it? Will there be more trouble?"

Alvin shrugged. "I don't know love. They fired Eustis, so I figured I'd see if Phillip would make good on his offer. Otherwise, I need to talk to Arthur and see what needs to happen next."

Mary sat back at first in disbelief then her face reddened as the anger welled with her. "We have a baby here Alvin. This can't become a feud."

"I know love. I won't let that happen."

"Da's going to be fit to be tied," said Kevin.

Alvin pulled his pipe from his pocket and lit it. "That he will. We'll need to be sure he sees reason."

Kevin laughed. "Ha! Good luck with that. He'll be out for blood."

Mary sat on the porch and watched her father sit and glare into the fire. She had heard his rage thousands of times, but his being silent was far more terrifying.

Alvin, Kevin and Eustis sat silently waiting for his response to the fight, when the silence was split by Arthur's bellow. "Son of a whore!" he stood and paced like a caged tiger Mary had seen at the circus once as a young girl. The beast was behind bars but still looked dangerous to her. So did Arthur.

"The LaCroix brothers pedal nearly a third of our business. If we can't sell to them, there is no expanding. Maybe that's what Moreland was up to all along."

Alvin tossed the end of his drink into the fire and a plume of flame shot into the air. "If we can't sell to them, then we'd have to sell to him and I'm certain he intends to dictate terms."

"Terms? I can tell you about his terms. He'll buy from us on the cheap because we have no other option. Then he'll either water it down so that nobody wants it or simply dump it on the ground and tell people in town it's his whiskey or nothing."

Kevin scoffed. "They won't buy it. They can't afford it."

"Oh really? If they want it, they'll pay. They'll starve their God damned families for that brown bottle, I can assure you." Arthur pointed to Alvin. "Ask him. He'll tell you. The village had children no bigger around than a twig for want of food and their father sitting right down at the pub about to fall off their feckin' stool."

Alvin looked at Kevin and nodded. "It's true. I wish it weren't, but your Da has the right of it."

"We could make an army from the east side of Howell Hill," said Kevin trying to offer something more than a fat lip and a blank stare.

Arthur contemplated on that for a moment. "And do what? We could certainly disrupt his business on this side of the mountain, but he'll have the police in his pocket the minute we cross the town line, and we'll all end up in jail. That won't work."

Mary could see that Alvin was working the various permutations over in his mind. Alvin stood and stretched his back as if he were trying to shed a great burden from his shoulders. "Let me talk to him. Find out what he's about and then we can make a plan from there."

Everyone nodded in agreement and Arthur spoke up. "I trust you son. But be leery. I've never seen such a change in a man, there's no predicting his mind."

Mary laid Alder in his crib and crept to the table without a sound. Alvin sat staring, contemplating his cup of tea and startled when she touched his shoulder.

"I'm sorry love," she whispered. "I just wanted you back from wherever your mind was."

Alvin reached over and slid his arm around her waist pulling her tight to him. "I'm right where I want to be now."

"Are you worried about Moreland?"

Alvin released his grip and sat back. "Not worried...he's always been civil with me. More contemplating strategy, I guess. He can't be bullied, he's too powerful for that. There has to be a way to appeal to his business sense." A grin crept across his face. "I just don't know enough about business to know what makes sense." Then he laughed softly at his play on words.

Mary shook her head and gave him a playful push. "You're a clever one alright. Too clever for your own good."

"Clever enough to land a beauty like you."

"Ha," scoffed Mary. "I landed you if I recall. You were so nervous I practically had to trick you into kissing me."

"It's not that I didn't want to. It's just your father can be a scary man."

Mary leaned in and kissed Alvin. "I think he's satisfied with how this all worked out. Your coming here was the best thing for all of us. I've never seen him happier."

Alvin stood and wrapped his arms around Mary and kissed her neck. She closed her eyes shuddered at the feel of goose-bumps running up her spine. He leaned back and looked her in the eyes with a soft grin. "Think the baby will be asleep for a while?"

"A couple hours at least."

Alvin slid his hands down her back and cupped he bottom in each hand, pulling her tightly against his pelvis. "It won't take that long, I promise. I couldn't last two hours."

Mary scoffed. "Well, you damned well better try. Charm only goes so far."

Thirty

Alvin sat on a bench outside of Parker's office at the More-land house. He could hear cooks busy in the kitchen and the smell of fresh baked bread wafted down the hall. He closed his eyes and tried to imagine it slathered in butter. The image was so real in his mind that it made his stomach rumble with envy.

The office door opened, and Hammond emerged and frowned like a petulant child at the sight of Alvin. His left eye was still swollen, but he could see out of it and his mouth was a tapestry of blue and purple where Omar his hit him with the first blow. "He'll see you now," Hammond said and walked out the front door without another word or so much as a glance at Alvin.

Alvin stood and took a deep breath, then exhaled. When he entered the room, Parker was standing beside his desk and walked forward to meet Alvin. Alvin was taken aback and tensed as if for a fight until Parker extended his hand.

"Thank you for coming," he said, and Alvin reached out and shook Parker's hand.

"Thanks for having me."

Parker motioned to a chair in front of the fire instead of across the desk. "Let's talk here. The doors are nice, but they make an uncomfortable draft on my back when I'm working." Parker opened a crystal decanter, not unlike the one at Richard's house in Ireland. "Can I interest you in a whiskey?"

Alvin sat frozen for a moment. He had come prepared for a fight and all of this civility had unmanned his resolve. Perhaps that was the intent, he thought. "Just a small one please, I still have work to do today."

Parker chuckled and poured two fingers of whiskey into a crystal glass and handed it to Alvin.

Alvin felt the weight of the glass and nodded with approval. "Nice crystal."

"Thank you. Comes from Waterford. From your part of the world. Have you ever been there?"

Alvin shook his head and took a sip of whiskey. The drink was smooth and smokey with a slight sweetness. "I haven't. Only been as far as Cork. It's about eighty miles from Waterford."

"Well, I've never been there either, but this is the finest crystal I have ever seen. My wife gave this to me for our first anniversary."

Alvin nodded with approval. "That's a fine gift."

"She was a fine woman." He paused and looked at the glass, then took a long drink and sat down in the chair on the opposite side of the fire. "Obviously I didn't invite you here to reminisce. I'd like to talk about this ugliness in town before things get out of hand."

"Agreed," Alvin said, then took another drink.

"Hammond told me his version. Perhaps, you'd share yours."

Alvin related the story exactly as he had for Mary and parker listened without reaction. He didn't frown, he didn't nod, he just listened. Alvin couldn't help but think that more people should study this man and his ability to take in information without becoming emotional.

When Alvin finished, Parker took another drink from his glass and stared at Alvin without speaking.

Alvin wondered if he was trying to melt him under the weight of his gaze, so he adopted the same demeanor that Parker had when Alvin told his story.

Parker grinned. "Well, that's more or less how Hammond told it. He left some parts out. But I'll deal with that later." Parker placed the glass on a small table beside his chair and opened a silver cigarette case, offering one to Alvin.

"Thank you. I will take one," Alvin said, and Parker leaned forward and held a small metal box in his hand. When he flicked the wheel with his thumb, a spark and then a flame arose. Alvin puffed at the flame with wide eyes. It was the first time he had ever seen someone light a cigarette without a match. "That's amazing."

Parker lit his own cigarette and chuckled. "It beats the hell out of matches."

Alvin drew in smoke and exhaled out of the side of his mouth. "I imagine it would."

Parker leaned back in his chair and crossed one leg over the other. "When I told you, you could expand, I was imagining that you'd be doing the selling, not the Lacroix's"

Alvin was a bit surprised by the comment. Parker knew their operation better than they knew his. "We don't sell directly in town. It takes too long to get there, and we have farms to tend. Besides, the LaCroix brothers already knew everyone."

Parker took another drag and contemplated on that for a moment. "That makes sense, I guess. But the issue is that Omar and his brothers are my direct competitors. If they sell in town, it makes it harder for us to sell in town. We already have all the taverns, but there's nothing else except the people they sell to."

Alvin could see his point. He liked Omar, but he could see how from a business perspective, having two outfits selling liquor would undoubtedly lead to confrontation at some point.

"Why don't you expand to other towns? Monroe only has so many taverns."

"Believe me. I've thought of that. The problem is a lack of supply. It might surprise you, but it's not easy to get liquor across the border in large quantities. At least not large enough to make it worth my while."

Alvin could see the problem with that. Small batches don't attract attention, that's why they only sell a handful of gallons at a time. He sipped his drink again and as he watched the golden liquid swirl around in his glass, he had an idea. "What if you bought from Omar?"

Parker stopped smoking for a minute and stared at Alvin with the same gaze he had used at the beginning of their meeting. "Why would he sell to me?"

Alvin's mind was racing though the possibilities and consequences of such an arrangement, and he worked fast to lay out a plan. "He has a supplier in Canada, same as you, but you get your liquor from the north, and he gets his from over the mountains in the west. I would assume they are different suppliers."

"They are."

"Well Omar buys whiskey in small quantities, sells them to make a little profit and buys some more. You have money. He doesn't. I can't speak for him of course, but if he were to get you more liquor, you could expand to other towns, and he could keep selling at the mill. He only buys what he can afford, but I think they have more to sell him if he had more money."

Now Alvin could see Parker working through the idea in his mind as he stared at the fire. After a few moments of silence, he nodded to himself as he arrived at acceptance.

"That is a very reasonable plan. Do you think he'd meet with me? I'd like to work out a strategy to distribute in Palmyra, Sparta and Brownfield Junction first, but this is worth discussing."

Alvin felt as though a weight had been lifted. "I don't know if he would here. But maybe if we met at my place and Arthur was there, we could all come to a lasting agreement."

Parker chuckled. "Oh yes. Your father-in-law. How'd he take the news of the fight?"

"He was as angry as I have ever seen him. Maybe even angrier than when I told him his daughter was with child, and it was mine."

Now Parker laughed out loud. "That angry? Maybe I should be the one nervous about meeting with them."

Alvin didn't think he was being serious, so he laughed along with him. "I think it's a reasonable plan and if he makes more money, so will Arthur."

"It is a reasonable plan. I hope LaCroix sees reason too."

"If he doesn't?"

Parker tossed his cigarette into the fire. "Then I'll simply ask that you and your family stay out of it. I like you, and I'd like to keep it that way."

Alvin smiled and extended his hand. "I like you too, and I want to keep it that way as well."

Parker stood and shook Alvin's hand. "Have you ever considered politics? You could probably run that town if you wanted. With my backing of course."

Alvin stood and smiled. "I'm a farmer. Animals are easier to tend than people. Besides, I have a stomach for shoveling shite, not listening to it."

This made Parker laugh and he started toward the door. When he reached the knob, he stopped and slipped his hand into his pocket producing a bundle of folded bills. He peeled off two fives and three one-dollar bills and handed them to Alvin.

"When you see Eustis, please tell him no hard feelings, and that's last weeks pay and this weeks. You'll see that he gets it?"

"I will. I promise."

"Eustis is a good man. I heard Phillip Armstrong had offered him a job."

"He did. At the Grange."

Parker nodded. "Well, he'd be one hell of a man in the woods."

"I'll Phillip know. Can I ask you a question? I don't want to give offense."

Parker stopped and studied Alvin, "go ahead."

"A lot of people wouldn't have paid him at all once they gave him the sacking. You paid him for time he didn't even work. Why?"

Parker smiled. "People say I'm a ruthless businessman. Which, when it comes to property and liquor, I am. But my father's men loved him. They loved him because he was a fair man to work for. Now Eustis will probably never work for me again, but he is a good man from a good family. It only cost me a couple of dollars to keep his respect and theirs. The Olivers have a big family with dozens of cousins and words spread fast around here. Good and bad. I'd rather have them talk good about us. That's the best money I've ever spent."

"Thank you. I appreciate you explaining. I'll see he gets the money."

Alvin stepped into the hallways and was about to leave when Parker called out. "Alvin. I heard your brother is coming from Ireland. When he gets here, bring him by. I'd like to meet him."

Alvin gave Parker a puzzled look. "How'd you know that?"

"I just told you. Words spread fast around here."

Thirty-One

Mary could only recall seeing Alvin truly excited on three occasions. When Richard came to visit, when he saw his family at Kellen's wedding and when Alder was born. Otherwise, he was a man of little emotion. He was loving and caring towards her, but nothing seemed to affect his mood to make him very excited.

Today, however, he was positively giddy. He paced the platform at the Watertown rail station and looked over the tree line for smoke. In his mind it was the surest way to know it was coming.

Mary bounced Alder in her arms to keep him happy while Alvin paced from one end of the landing to the other. "You're too nervous," she said. "The train will be here any moment. Trains are very punctual you know."

Alvin stopped and checked his watch. "I can't remember if I wound this or not. It may be off, you know. It loses time when I forget to wind it."

Mary chuckled, "I'm sure it's fine. If we lost time, then we would be late and obviously we're not. There's no train here."

Alvin stopped pacing and contemplated on that for a minute. "I suppose you're right."

"I know I am. I'm always right."

Alvin shook his head then jumped and turned back to the trees. "Shh! Hear that?"

Mary listened intently, but she didn't hear anything. "It's the wind."

"Bah. You're not right about this. I hear the rumble of the train, and I can feel it in my shoes."

Mary listened harder and then she felt like she could feel a slight vibration in the platform. A moment later she saw the plume of smoke rising above the trees.

Alvin thrust his finger toward the tree line. "There! See it!"

"Well even a blind squirrel finds an acorn sometimes." Mary said laughing.

The smoke rolled closer, and she could feel the rumble of the train. When the whistle blew, Alder startled and began to cry. The big black locomotive rounded the bend and made its way to the platform.

Alvin put his watch in his pocket and straightened his clothes.

"Relax Alvin. It's your brother, not the Pope."

Alvin ignored the comment and stood straight and proud.

Train screeched as it came to stop and let out a long, loud hiss as the steam was released from the tank. People streamed out of the cars line ants from a hill. Alvin scanned the riders looking for a familiar face, but it was Mary who saw him first.

"Well now. Young McGinn. Is that yourself?" she said with a laugh.

Alvin spun around and saw his brother Jameson standing before her holding a single bag.

He was much taller than Mary had remembered, and he was rail thin. Jameson had the same square jaw as Alvin and a thick mass of brown hair. His eyes were dark brown and reminded Mary of dog's eyes. "Hug your brother or meet your nephew. Your choice."

Jameson smiled at Alvin and made his way to Mary and Alder. "Him, I've seen before." Jerking a thumb toward Alvin. "But this is my first nephew."

Jameson took Alder and held him close kissing his cheek. "He looks like you love."

"Well. You never know what you're going to get," said Alvin. "I'm just glad he didn't look like Kellen."

Jameson handed the baby back to Mary and turned to his brother. "Thank you for bringing me over."

Alvin hugged Jameson's skinny frame and lifted him off the ground. "I'm glad you're here. I thought they'd never let you come." Then he placed him on the ground.

Jameson shrugged. "Da would have let me go back with you and Kellen, but Ma didn't. Now she wanted me gone before I get mixed up in the troubles. There's talk of rebellion against the English. Lot's of whispering at the pubs. It's not good."

"Well please don't talk to my father about it," said Mary. "He'll rale on for hours about all the injustices brought on by the English."

Jameson smiled. "I won't talk about it. I'm happy to be away from it for a while. That's all they ever talk about now."

Alvin pulled his pipe from his pocket and lit a match. "Was Emily disappointed you left?"

"Not as much as you would think. She's on about Oisin O' Malley day and night. He's so smart. He's so handsome. Bit of a Nancy boy if you ask me. He's learnin' the tailor trade. Making suits and the like."

Mary scowled. "That takes skill and years of practice. It doesn't make him a Nancy."

Alvin smiled and put his arm around her. "Easy love. He means nothing by it. It's hard to explain. In Ireland, a man who digs ditches for a living is held in more esteem than an educated man among the common folk. I imagine it's because what they do is real. They can see it and touch it. Most of them have done it."

"I wouldn't care if you were a farmer or a banker. I'd love you either way," she said.

Alvin smiled and pointed at Mary. "See this one here? When you want to settle down, this is what you look for and remember this. It doesn't matter how a man makes a living, as long as he earns it."

Jameson picked up his bag. "I know. Da had said that to me about a half a thousand times. Now, where's this farm of yours?"

"About two hours by wagon. Maybe it's a bit longer. It rained yesterday, so the roads are still a little soft."

Jameson inspected the wagon and nodded with approval. "Well, that looks faster than a donkey cart. Can you show me how to drive the horses?"

Alvin helped Mary into the wagon bed, and she settled onto the back bench with Alder cradled in her arms. He pointed to the driver's bench and smiled. "No time like now to learn. Jump up."

Jameson climbed up and took the reins in his hands. "Are they hard to steer?"

Alvin sat down and lit his pipe again. "Just get them started and they know the way."

Jameson studied the long thongs of leather trying to imagine what to do with them. "Do I snap their backsides with these?"

"No, that'll just make them irritable. They listen for sounds." Alvin made two louds clicks with is tongue and shouted. "Let's go!" Chum and Pal leaned into the load and strained against the weight of the wagon. "Oh, release the brake to your right."

Jameson pushed a long metal lever ahead and the wagon started rolling forward. "That's better."

The wagon bumped along and Mary listening as Jameson filled Alvin in on all the gossip in the village. Paddy Collins was doing well and sends his regards. His sons bought a boat of their own and Paddy hired a local lad as big as Kellen to work on the Ellen Marie and the boys named their boat Edna's Robin.

The money brokers are now just called Wilkes and Company. It seems that Booth had not only swindled people in the village but had stolen money from his Lordship as well.

When Lord Ellingwood's accountants discovered the theft and what had been happening in the village, he had Booth arrested and tried in Ireland. He was sent to Cork Gaol for two years, but they reduced it to one when he paid Richard back. Richard made things right in the village and split the money up among all those who had been cheated. "Cork was full of hard men and Booth is soft. Everyone says it will go poorly for him there," said Jameson.

Carrigan had died from the drink and Nero or as Jameson preferred, Kelly went to the next farm over and tended the flock there.

Mary had heard Alvin tell so many stories about the village, she felt as though she could picture every person, and every place Jameson spoke about. The fishing lane, the docks, even Carrigan's farm. They all felt like places she knew.

As they made the big turn toward Howell Hill Road, Jameson sat up straight and pointed. "Is that the lord's house?"

Alvin laughed. "I asked the same thing myself. No. It's the Moreland's house. They just act like they're lords. But they hold no titles."

"And money. Lots of it," added Mary. "Your brother was in that house not two days ago."

"What were you doing there?"

"Negotiating with the devil," replied Alvin with a laugh.

Mary shook her head. "He's not that bad. There was a time when he was your friend."

"I believe that we are still friends. He's not a bad man. He's just misunderstood."

Jameson shifted on the bench trying to get more comfortable. "Why is he misunderstood?"

"Moreland doesn't like to lose. If he wants something, he tends to get it. That's why it's good you're here. To help us keep a farm from falling into Moreland hands."

Jameson chuckled. "They must not have heard of the famous McGinn stubbornness."

Alvin leaned backward to stretch his muscles. "Believe me. He's learning. he wants to meet you once your settled."

Mary frowned. "What on earth for?"

"I don't know. Just to meet him, I guess. Like I said, I believe we're still friends."

Thirty–Two

A lvin, Jameson and Omar sat on the porch drinking coffee as the sun rose well above the horizon. It was warm enough so that you couldn't see your breath, and the sunlight felt good on Alvin's face.

The trees were all bare, but birds still flitted about from limb to limb. He smiled when he heard the Cardinal's song and watched at two bright males competed for the lone tan female sitting on a branch below.

"That's my favorite bird," he said pointing at the bare apple tree in the yard.

"The red ones?" asked Jameson.

"Yes. Those are the males. The female is the tan one with the bright orange beak."

Omar scoffed. "A cardinal is fine, but the Blue Jay is a more impressive bird."

Their bird debate was interrupted by the rumble of a horse and carriage turning into the dooryard. Parker sat beside a driver, not Hammond, but someone Alvin didn't recognize. That's good, he thought. Hammond's presence might have disrupted the whole proceeding.

The carriage stopped and Parker stepped out. "Stay with the carriage," he said to the driver and pulled a bottle of whiskey from a leather bag in the back. "Good morning. Where's your father-in-law?"

Alvin stepped down from the porch and shook his hand. "On his way back from his place. He took Mary and the baby there for the morning. He fusses a lot when he's hungry, so we thought it better if they went there."

Parker laughed. "Hub is miserable with his teeth cutting through. The nursemaid rubbed whiskey on his gums, but it doesn't seem to help. I think he just likes the whiskey."

Alvin could see Arthur returning and pointed. "Here he comes. Do you want to go inside or wait?"

Parker looked and saw Arthur was no great way off and shrugged. "I don't mind; we can wait."

Alvin had the feeling that Arthur was being deliberately slow to ensure that Moreland had to wait on him instead of the reverse.

Parker stepped to LaCroix with his hand extended, "Omar. Where are your brothers?"

Omar reached out cautiously and shook his hand. "They're busy. But I speak for all three of us."

There was tension between them that Alvin could feel in his gut. Any attempt by Moreland to apologize for the fight in the mill yard, would ring hollow, so he searched his mind for something to keep the conversation civil. He saw Jameson standing at the edge of the porch and smiled.

"Parker. This is my brother Jameson. Just arrived from Ireland."

Parker released LaCroix's hand and stepped to the porch. "So, this is the young man everyone is talking about. The one all the local girls are so anxious to meet."

Jameson looked completely befuddled. "They are?"

"He's just pulling your leg," said Alvin.

"He hasn't touched my leg."

Alvin laughed. "It's an expression they use here to say he's having a bit of fun with you."

"Oh." Jameson frowned.

"That's not true," said Parker. "The bunkhouse gossips more than a group of old women and they're all jealous of the brother of the Irishman McGinn."

"I never even met them. Why are they jealous?"

Parker patted him on the shoulder. "It's nothing to worry about. They're all envious of Alvin because he married McCall's daughter. They figure the girls will all be after you next."

The conversation was halted by the sound of Arthur rumbling into the yard. "Jameson. Can you come hitch my wagon for me?"

"I can," he said with a broad smile and jumped down the steps rushing to the horse. Jameson enjoyed the animals and was always anxious at any chance to be around them.

"He likes the horses him?" asked Omar.

Alvin smiled. "He does now. Wait until that little gray bastard in the barn takes a chomp at him. He won't like that one."

***

The four men sat at the table while Jameson say on a chair next to the kitchen stove. Alvin produced four glasses and a tin cup, from the cabinet. "May I?" he asked Parker.

"Yes please. That's what I brought it for."

Alvin poured some whiskey into each glass and a small amount into the cup. He brought the tin cup to Jameson and leaned in speaking softly. "Just sip it and just listen."

Jameson grinned and nodded, taking the cup and sitting it in his lap.

He could still feel the tension between Parker and Omar and Arthur seemed to be less boisterous than usual. So, Alvin walked back to the table and stood with his cup held up in front of him. "Can we have a toast together for luck before we start?"

The men rose slowly and held out their glasses. Alvin looked at each one in turn, then spoke. "May you live as long as you want and never want as long as you live. Slainte."

They men all smiled and drank before retaking their seats. Alvin laid out the broader points of his discussion with Parker and opened the table for anyone to speak.

Parker spoke first, "My problem is getting enough of it over the border. The police there expect a percentage on both sides of the border and by the time I've paid them and the Sheriff's deputies, it makes a deep cut into my margins."

Omar nodded and frowned. "Same. Except I can get it over without paying, but to sell it, I have to pay the police chief, the foot officers, and the mill yard manager. They all get paid before I see a nickel. Police are the biggest thieves of all."

Alvin chuckled, "See, you have that in common."

Parker studied Omar for a moment. "How do you get it over without paying?"

"Woodlots on the border. We set up one on our side and then they set up one across the border in Canada, when we're ready to leave, they just walk it across and we pay them. We bring it out with the wood."

Parker seemed to weigh that in his mind as he sipped his whiskey. "Seems like a lot of work for twenty gallons of whiskey."

Omar chuckled. "It would be, but we aren't the only ones. Buyers come from all down the Western mountains. Some nearly a hundred miles."

Parker placed his glass down on the table. "How much could they sell us?"

Omar chuckled. "I never thought of it as us before." He scratched his head and shrugged. "A wagon load. Maybe two, but I don't know how they'd supply all of the other buyers."

A small grin crept across Parker's face. "We'll pay more."

Omar shook his head. "If I pay more, I'll make nothing."

Parker thought about that for a moment. "Look. You pay your normal amount to me. I'll see to it that the police in Monroe are taken care of out of my money. Plus, I'll give you and your brothers one case each for the risk of getting it over the border of the woods."

Omar sat back and studied Moreland as he calculated the deal in his head. "Why are you so generous to me? I thought you wanted us out of the way."

He pointed at Alvin. "You can thank your friend here. If you think that deal is generous, then I'm happy. You'll make more money, and I'll make more money, much more."

"If I refuse?"

Parker held his hands out as if to say, I don't know. "Then our next encounter might not be as joyous. But I think this plan benefits us both."

Omar sat and stared at Parker and Parker stared back. Both men expressionless and Alvin felt it getting harder to breathe with the tension in the air.

Arthur banged his glass down on the table. "For Christ's sake Omar, even I think that's a fair deal."

Omar looked at Arthur and smiled. "Me too." He looked back at Parker. "Drink on it?"

Parker stood and smiled. "Shake on it first, and then we'll drink."

Parker and Omar shook hands and Alvin refilled the glasses. He walked over to Jameson who was still sitting silently and poured some more whiskey into his cup. He smiled and gave Jameson a wink.

Jameson smiled back and sipped his whiskey.

"I saw Hartley's place on the way by. It looks good," said Parker.

Alvin nodded and smiled. "It's been a struggle, but he's home now."

"I saw tree length wood in the yard. Is that his firewood or is he selling that?"

Alvin's face fell a little. "Firewood. We got a late start on getting it. We're going to have a wood party on Sunday. Try to get it finished before the snow flies."

Parker finished his drink and sat the glass on the table. "I'll send the bunkhouse over for the afternoon after they're done tending the animals."

Alvin looked down at the floor, then back to Parker. "Hartley's got no money, and we can't really pay them either."

"Pay them in food and drink. I'll give them a couple extra dollars in their pay this week."

Alvin smiled and shook Parker's hand. "Thank you. That's greatly appreciated."

Parker turned to Jameson before leaving and shook his hand, then pointed to Alvin. "It's been nice meeting you. If you want to be a man of great character someday, learn from this man."

"I will."

Thirty-Three

The sun was as high as it would get on a November day, and Mary watched in amazement as the yard buzzed with activity. Teams of men sawed the logs and as soon as it hit the ground another man brought it to the blocks for splitting. Once the sticks were split, Jameson collected them in wheelbarrows and brought them to the long shed that ran between the house and the barn, where Alvin piled them neatly into long rows that ran the length of the barn. *This must be what it looks like inside of an ant hill*, she thought. *All working to accomplish a common task.*

Mary held the kitchen door and Julia stepped out with an enormous ham from the house and placed it on a makeshift table made from sawhorses and planks. The ham was surrounded by biscuits, butter, boiled potatoes, carrots and turnips. At the far end of the table sat two large ceramic jugs of cider. Alvin insisted on sweet cider until the work was done. Hard cider would only lead to slower work and the possibility of someone chopping off their own toes if they missed with an axe.

"Wash up and come eat!" she called from the porch and the din of sawing and splitting wood quieted to happy voices and shuffling feet.

Alvin emerged from the barn and stopped at the water pump to wash. He pumped the long handle three times and water flowed into a bucket that hung below the spigot. When he was satisfied that he had enough, he plunged his hand in and splashed his face to clear away the dirt. He walked to Mary with water still dripping down his face and when he hugged her, he wiped his face on her shawl.

The men heaped their plates with food and made their way anywhere they could sit and eat. Moreland had sent over four men, and Hammond was not one of them. This made her happy, there would be less likelihood of any leftover hostilities from their encounter a couple weeks earlier. As she surveyed the men, shy chuckled softly to herself.

"What's so funny," asked Alvin.

Mary motioned her head to what she was looking at. Eustis was sitting in the middle of the four Moreland men and looked like a giant next to them. They were all of an average size, but Eustis' broad chest and shoulders were as wide as any two of the others put together.

He had spent the morning on a two man saw with Phillip to see how they might work together. Eustis may not have been overly bright, but he was very good at following instructions and never seemed to tire on the saw.

Alvin smiled. "He does make a sight to behold. Can't miss him, that's for sure."

"Dammit." Mary sputtered.

"What's wrong?"

"I should have invited Norma Bean to come. The next time he sees her will probably be at another dance and who knows if he will come after the way he was treated at the last one."

Alvin plucked a biscuit from the table and smeared a healthy portion of butter into the center. "It's not really a great day for courting, unless she wants to take Phillip's place," he said with a mocking grin.

Mary could see the logic in that. "Well, we should have her over next Sunday for dinner, I'll have one of the boys drop by with a message next time they go to Hemmings'."

"Perhaps you've missed your calling. You're a natural *Babhdior*," he said with a smile and kissed her on the cheek, then wiped off the excess butter that clung to it.

"What on earth is that?" she asked and wiped her cheek again to make sure it was all gone.

"It is Gaelic, it means matchmaker."

Mary scoffed. "I highly doubt that's my calling. But I do think that they would be good for each other."

Alvin tried to recall what she looked like and remembered how Mary had said they called her Pole Bean. "I imagine if they ever had children, they would be very tall and very thin."

Mary scoffed at this too. "Nonsense. They'd be average height and average weight. I learned that in Animal Husbandry when I was in school. If you mate two large animals, you'll get large offspring. Two small animals, small offspring. But a large and a small, chances are that you'll get average."

"How do you explain your brother Daniel then? He's bigger than Arthur."

"I suppose there's the off chance of a big one or a small one."

Alvin laughed. "Alder looks to be of average size. I wonder what the next one will be."

Mary smiled and took his hand. "I guess you'll see next summer."

Alvin froze with a half-eaten biscuit clutched in his left hand as his mind worked through what he had just heard. "Next summer you say?"

Mary nodded and studied his face to see if he would be happy or upset. When she saw his mouth change to a big toothy smile, she squeezed his hand. "We'll have a sister for Alder."

"Are you positive? I thought a woman couldn't get pregnant when she was breast feeding."

Mary laughed. "I think that's an old wife's tale. Besides, how else could you explain so many Irish twins?"

"I'm overjoyed love. Does anyone else know?"

"Just my mother."

"Can I tell people?"

Mary leaned in and kissed him on the cheek. "Tell whoever you want."

Alvin took a deep breath and smiled. "Hey Arthur! I have some news!"

From the Author: Alvin's Journey

When I finished the fourth and final book in the McGinn Family Saga, readers asked if I would keep going. But I felt that rather than continuing that story line, it might be more interesting to go back to the beginning of Alvin and Mary, along with the adult characters who featured prominently in the McGinn books.

The numerous bird references stemmed from research on a single Irish superstition about closing the doors when you move so that bad luck can't follow you. This is where not writing from a plot allows me to take the characters down different paths than intended when something interesting emerges from research.

The period of time between 1905 and 1933 (when The Red Road begins) is rich with amazing historical events and will be the basis of a new series that picks up where the Cardinal's Song ends. The Monroe Chronicles (as the series will be called) will cover events like World War I, the Spanish influenza pandemic, women's right to vote and of course prohibition and the great depression, with other events of the times sprinkled in. I hope that you will continue to keep following the McGinns and watch with me as the children grow up.

Thank you for your continued support and I look forward to bringing you new work in 2026.

Go raibh mile maith agat (May you have a thousand goodnesses)

ALSO BY

The McGinn Family Saga

The Red Road
The Mothers McGinn
Counting Crossroads
The Warrior's Wounds

Alvin's Journey

The Robin's Gaze
The Blue Jay's Call
The Cardinal's Song